# ZOMBIES
## versus
# ALIENS

### Aaron Thibault

RING
WYRM
BOOKS

First Edition

ISBN-13: 978-0692871706
ISBN-10: 0692871705

# ZOMBIES

*versus*

# ALIENS

# PROLOGUE

The slow drift through space ended. The pods, a mix of technology and biology, touched the planet's atmosphere, and the friction set the outer layer on fire. Some of the pods disintegrated, their occupants dying without even realizing it. But the rest hurtled down to the surface and, perhaps, a new future.

The stars shined in the sky over the Mojave Desert just as they have for countless ages.

Joaquin strolled slowly down the middle of the single lane highway, enjoying the still air and the evening heat. His truck was about a mile down the road. It still worked, but Joaquin needed to make this trip by himself. Needed to hear the sound of his boots on the road and to feel the air that was no different than it was fifteen years ago.

A giant sandstone rock, the only prominent feature along the highway, marked Joaquin's destination. The rock stood about twenty feet tall and reached about forty feet wide. It was not a huge rock compared to the standards of the California deserts, but it was enough to hide a group of killers.

Joaquin found the spot he was looking for without thinking. Its location was burned into his mind, part of a terrible memory that he never wanted to think about but he never wanted to forget. It was on this spot, fifteen years ago tonight, that Lara died. Or, as Joaquin had prayed every night since, he hoped she had died.

The war started five weeks before that time. It started with the explosions, high up in the sky. Scientists said Earth just passed through a cloud of space dust. There was nothing to worry about. Then the killings started. The first week, everyone dismissed it as an elaborate hoax. A media panic. Political scaremongering. The entire idea reeked with absurdity. The reports of a sudden rise in cannibal murders sounded too stupid to believe. It was just bath salts or synthetic marijuana Joaquin told Lara.

On the second week, they heard about the bodies coming back from the dead. Everyone still thought is was a hoax, but the emergency sirens seemed to go on twenty-four hours a day. TV and radio service was dodgy at best. Apparently, everyone decided to use up their vacation days that week. And Mr. McAllister on the corner who normally tended his garden every morning? No one had seen him in a week. "The Patels are moving," Joaquin remarked to Lara. "Amazing that they could sell their house so fast in this economy."

At the end of that second week, Joaquin knew that zombies were real. The first time Lara said that word out loud to him, he laughed it off. The second time, he chuckled. The third time, he wished he had never sold his dad's old guns.

The enormity of the situation hit home in a rare moment when the TV stations were operational. The news helicopter hovered over downtown Los Angeles, aiming its camera at thousands of people running wildly through the streets. He couldn't tell which ones were human and which were zombies, but he could see all the blood and bodies and pieces of bodies strewn across the streets. Sometimes the camera would focus on a single person getting torn to shreds by a group of zombies. The reporter and the TV audience just watched in silence. There were no words that could describe the feeling of knowing that the end of the world just started.

During one especially brutal murder, Joaquin turned away from the TV and looked outside the window. The day was normal, beautiful even, except for the thick column of smoke rising from just over the horizon. Downtown LA.

When he turned back to the TV, the camera focused on the entrance to one of the skyscrapers. Zombies by the hundreds forced their way into the building. It kind of looked like one of those Black Friday viral videos, Joaquin thought. Then he wondered, how could I be so morbid?

The news reporter explained the situation, but Joaquin didn't listen. He knew exactly what happened. When all the people in the skyscraper saw the violence in the streets, they were faced with a choice. Fight your way to freedom or hide. They chose to hide, and the zombies found them. They trapped themselves in that skyscraper, an easy feast for the zombies. Trapped by their own inaction.

And Joaquin had no intentions of letting that happen to him and Lara. Twenty minutes later, their SUV was packed, and they were on their way.

It was another few weeks of fighting and killing and crying before Joaquin, Lara, and a small group of other survivors were walking along a lonely highway in the middle of the Mojave Desert. There weren't too many people in the desert, so it had to be the safest place to live.

That mentality got Lara killed. The group walked past a large piece of sandstone, not thinking that there could be any threat in the desert. Joaquin and Lara took up the rear. Just as they passed the large rock, the zombies jumped out from hiding. They grabbed Lara first, and they almost got Joaquin, but he tripped over his own feet and out of their grasp.

A zombie lumbered over Joaquin, hunger burning in its dead eyes. Joaquin pulled out his revolver and filled the night air with the zombie's rotting brains. The body slumped to the floor as chunks of its head rained down on Joaquin. He scrambled to his feet, pointing the gun at Lara's attackers. The hammer fell on an empty chamber. He had used his last bullet to save himself.

Flaps of skin hung loosely from the bite marks across Lara's arms. Her jaw was missing, but the tongue still waggled as Lara attempted to scream. In her one remaining eye, Joaquin saw the most intense fear and pain he could possibly imagine. Despite her injuries, Lara still fought to get away from the zombies.

Joaquin decided that she would not die alone. He flipped his revolver around to use it like a club and charged into battle. A pair of hands wrapped around him and pulled him away. He readied himself for the feel of teeth sinking into his skin, but instead he heard a voice in his ear. "She's gone."

It was one of the other members of the group, dragging him to safety. Lara was lost, and there were too many zombies to fight. So they ran away. They ran through the night and all of the next day. And the whole time, Joaquin prayed to God, someone he had not spoken to in a long time, that Lara died before turning into one of those things.

The memory was still fresh in Joaquin's mind. The stench of decaying bodies, the wheezing of air through desiccated lungs. Every detail remembered perfectly. Even the sickness in his gut when he realized his wife had been taken away from him.

But it was war. The war. People died. And if Lara had not died, Joaquin would never have met Becky. Grief and anger and hatred buried Joaquin in a hole so dark and deep he could not see the sky. He was ready to join Lara. But Becky pulled him out. Despite losing her husband and son, Becky always looked toward that day when the war would end. And she taught Joaquin how to do that, too.

Together, they fought like hell to survive the zombies. And after those five long years of war, they fought like hell to make the world right again. And through it all, they loved each other. Sure, it was a love born out of desperation between two people who would never have noticed each other in a sane world, but it was strong, and it was good. And it carried both of them forward. And Becky knew that was the only direction that led away from the war.

But Becky, who fought all the sorrow and death and won, couldn't fight and win against a drunk driver. All of Joaquin's prayers to keep his new wife alive did nothing.

Now, Joaquin was alone in the middle of the desert, just as he was alone in the world. He drew his revolver, the same revolver that had been with him during the war, and pointed it at the spot where Lara's head would have been all those years ago. I should've saved her, he thought.

He opened the cylinder. He had just one bullet. Like on that night. Just one bullet. Letting out a heavy sigh, Joaquin closed the cylinder and pulled back on the hammer.

A shooting star streaked across the sky, followed closely by another. For a moment, Joaquin watched, marvelling at the beauty of nature. Several more shot through space, leaving trails of stardust. Then one passed so close to Joaquin that it lit up the sky as if it were daylight.

The shock wave from its crash landing knocked Joaquin off his feet. A thunderous roar followed, briefly leaving Joaquin with only the sound of a screaming whistle in his ears. When his head cleared, another meteorite hurtled out of the sky. Joaquin prepared for impact, but the second one was far enough away that the only thing he heard was a thunderous crack.

When the war started, Joaquin thought it was all a joke. He had no idea what the meteorites were, but he was not the same man today as he was those many years past.

He checked his gun. Still just one bullet. The rest were back in his truck.

# CHAPTER ONE

The airplane dipped as it made its final approach. Dr. Fiona Todd grabbed her armrests and pressed her back into her seat. She had never flown before, and the experience was more stressful than she had anticipated. The plane leveled off, but Fiona held her breath for a few moments longer than necessary.

Outside the window, the skyscrapers of downtown Los Angeles jutted out of the landscape, surrounded by green fields. After the war, there wasn't enough people to use all the abandoned houses, so survivors transformed the land into farms. And the aqueduct brought in more than enough water, considering the decrease in population. Downtown itself was untouched and abandoned. It served as some kind of shrine to the memory of the old world, the world before the war.

The ruins of the past and the beginnings of tomorrow, thought Fiona. The war ended ten years ago, but humanity was only getting back on its feet now. And nothing made the slowness of rebuilding more apparent than the refugee city beyond downtown and the farms.

Nestled against the hills, the refugee city should have been called quarantine city. After the war, people naturally wanted to go home or find someplace they thought they could make a new life. But everyone else was still paranoid and feared another outbreak of zombies, so the refugees ended up in camps.

And as the years passed and no one cleared the refugees of disease, the camps turned into cities. And they stayed that way. Top men worried that if all the refugees were let out, they would disrupt the fledgling economy. So every major city around the world ended up with their own refugee city.

Fiona wondered if her parents were in one of those refugee cities somewhere in the world. They went on vacation for their anniversary, and once the war started, they couldn't come back. And that was the last she knew about them. She dismissed the thoughts. Everyone wondered the same thing about their missing family and friends. It was easier to think that than the more reasonable answer. They fell victim to the undead.

But despite her own feelings, she couldn't imagine the anguish the refugees must have felt. They survived five years of zombies only to get trapped in quarantine for the next ten.

The plane dipped again, and the captain said something over the loudspeaker that Fiona couldn't hear. The descent continued, the wind rushing over the wings getting louder and louder, until the plane touched down. The forces acting on the plane rattled the machine, and Fiona waited for everything to break apart around her. Instead, they arrived safely.

Fiona quickly checked her backpack to make sure she had everything before disembarking. It was all there, including the packet from Dr. Cheung.

Dr. Robert Cheung was the hero of the war. He invented the weapon that killed zombies en masse without harming humans. His efforts saved the world. And he was Fiona's mentor.

They met after the war, and he encouraged Fiona to pursue molecular biology. But then he disappeared. Everyone speculated that the fame became too much for him, and he became a hermit. Fiona started thinking that, too, but then his letter arrived in the mail.

The letter was intentionally vague, but it indicated that Dr. Cheung was in some kind of trouble. Fiona also received a few security cards and instructions to steal something.

At first, the audacity of the request made her laugh. It had to be a joke. But something, a nagging in her brain or just gut instincts, told her that the letter was real. And that Dr. Cheung's request was serious.

When Fiona first met Dr. Cheung, the first thing she noticed was his scars. A pink and white ocean of chaotic waves. They started at his neck and went under his collar to reemerge at his wrists. Fiona imagined that the scars across his body were even worse. And she knew the cause, though she never knew anyone to survive it.

Sometimes, a zombie would become so rotten that its jaws didn't work anymore. It still had the desire to eat, it just couldn't rip away flesh with its mouth. So it dug its nails into a person's skin and tried to rip away as much as it could. And sometimes a whole horde of zombies would just come at a person, clawing and tearing. And somehow, Dr. Cheung lived through the pain and trauma.

When asked about the scars, Dr. Cheung's only response was "Some of us are lucky that the only scars we carry are on our body."

But Fiona was not one of those lucky people. She did things during the war that still haunted her nightmares. Once in a while, she had to remind herself that what she did wasn't murder or that some people deserved death more than others. Back then, she was a teenager and couldn't expect herself to have a clear moral compass. But she still felt shame. While Dr. Cheung rose up and created something that ended the war and saved humanity, she sank to the lowest levels of cruelty and violence, just like everybody else.

She didn't know what she would accomplish by following Dr. Cheung's letter. But if he asked for help, especially after hiding for so many years, then he really needed help. Fiona thought that maybe this would be her contribution to the rebuilding of the world.

The plane landed in Long Beach. The port made Long Beach the economic hub of Southern California, and over the past few years it became the major population center of the west coast. Fiona found a taxi and took it north towards Westwood and her destination, an army base.

She was a little nervous about sticking out, but what she saw mitigated her fears. There were plenty of civilians walking around, and based on the number of lab coats, many were either physicians or scientists. The rest must have been there for the job opportunities afforded by the military base.

Dr. Cheung's instructions directed her towards the hospital, and from there she had to find the lab. She walked into the hospital easily enough, but she didn't get too far before a soldier stopped her.

"Excuse me, ma'am," he said. "I need to see your ID." He held his rifle casually, but his finger was suspiciously close to the trigger.

Fiona tried to put on her best smile while she rummaged through her backpack. "Of course," she said. "I'm new here, and I don't really know what I'm doing." It was the most convincing excuse she could think of. She handed the guard the ID supplied to her from Dr. Cheung's letter.

The soldier studied the ID for a while, too long for Fiona's liking. It was as if he were trying to memorize all the details. He flashed her a smile and handed back the ID. "I know precisely where you need to go, ma'am." He gave her directions that matched the one's from the letter.

Fiona mumbled her thanks and hurried off. She kept her head down, but tried to keep her footsteps at a normal pace. She had a sense that the guard didn't trust her. Of course, if he didn't, he would have taken her down on the spot, but that didn't reassure Fiona.

It didn't matter. She just had to walk into the lab, steal one vial, and be off. It would take a minute at most. She would be gone, and the guard would forget her. Easy.

She reached the entrance to the lab, and to her dismay, it was an elevator instead of a regular door. And the only button next to the elevator pointed down. There was a guard station next to the elevator, but it was empty. That set off enough alarms in Fiona's head to make her want to turn around and leave.

She cursed herself for being too eager to help Dr. Cheung. She didn't really owe him anything. And whatever she wanted to atone for in her past was over. She wasn't special. During the war, everyone crossed boundaries they wouldn't have crossed in normal times. What made this so important to her?

Several booted footsteps echoed down the hall. A pair of soldiers turned the corner, and Fiona rushed to the elevator. She slid her ID card through a security scanner and hit the down button. The elevator door opened instantly. She stepped inside, and the elevator rolled down its shaft.

The descent seemed to take forever and proved more nerve-wracking than the descent in the airplane. But it gave Fiona time to think. She realized why she was doing what she did. It wasn't atonement or some way to return a favor to Dr. Cheung. She needed to prove to herself that she deserved to survive the war. That she could do something worthwhile with her life. Since the end, she'd always felt that she wasn't doing enough to justify her survival. She was doing this for herself, even if she didn't know what she was doing.

The elevator slowed and bumped to a halt. Before the doors even opened, the smell creeping through the seam told Fiona she just made a mistake. The reek of rotten flesh, foul and intoxicating, invaded Fiona's nose. It was a smell engrained in her memory.

The doors opened, and Fiona stepped into the laboratory. Zombies paced and moaned mindlessly in examination chambers separated from the rest of the lab by glass partitions. Dozens of them. Fiona could feel their stink soaking into her clothes and skin and hair. And their cries, sounding as if the humans hidden inside the zombies struggled to break out, brought back all the terrible memories.

She didn't even know she stumbled until the floor slammed into her knees. "This . . . this is impossible," she muttered. What was Dr. Cheung working on? Why were there zombies? Why weren't they all exterminated?

"It's not impossible," said a voice. It was a man's voice.

Fiona looked around the lab for someone, a human.

"Not there," said the voice. "In here."

Fiona looked up and found the source of the voice. One of the cells held a man and not a zombie. He quickly pulled on a long-sleeved shirt, but Fiona saw the scars. They weren't the kind of scars that Dr. Cheung had. They were bite marks. The man had been bitten by zombies, but he wasn't one of them.

"How is this possible?" Fiona asked.

He remained expressionless, but Fiona sensed an anger inside of him hot enough to melt the glass that separated them. But the voice that came out of him was almost sad. "I wish I knew."

# CHAPTER TWO

Sensors within the pod indicated that the surrounding earth had cooled enough to make it safe to climb out. The onboard computer sent an electric spark into the Vicious One's brain, awakening it from hibernation.

The body awoke first and tested out the gravity and air pressure of the planet. The body adjusted fluid pressures within itself to compensate for the differences between this planet and the space vessel where it had spent its entire life. It next detected that the atmosphere consisted mostly of nitrogen, with a not insignificant amount of oxygen and some carbon and other elements. Already, the body could sense the oxygen damaging its cells, so it adjusted its chemical balances to make use of the abundant nitrogen.

The body, content that it had done what it could to protect itself from the alien environment, brought the mind into consciousness.

The Vicious One felt no difference between the new planet and its normal home. It quickly perused the readouts in its pod. Satisfied that there were no immediate threats, it set the self-destruct timer and crawled out of the pod.

It found itself at the bottom of a long shaft with only a small glimpse of sunlight at the top. The pod had dug itself deep into the ground for protection, and the sides of the shaft were glassy smooth where the pod melted its way into the ground.

The Vicious One's claws sank easily into the glass, making the climb out into the world effortless. It emerged inside the pod's impact crater, where molten rock still cooled. The crater spanned nearly sixteen body lengths, indicating that the impact would have been enough for any reasonably advanced intelligence to detect. The Vicious One spoke to the gods, begging them for reassurance that the plague had eliminated any intelligence on the planet.

It waited several seconds, but its gods did not feel like listening this moment.

The sun beat down on the Vicious One, and in response to the damage from the ultraviolet light, its carapace released an oily substance for protection. All of the Vicious One's practice missions had been on planets without an atmosphere, and the strangeness of the blue sky tried to distract it from its mission.

A strong hiss, escaping from within the shaft, brought the Vicious One back into reality. The self-destruct on the pod had activated, releasing acid that now ate through the pod.

The terrain around the crater was flat and so dry the sand felt like rock, yet vegetation still managed to grow. It was the desert, just as the strategists had told the Vicious One before sending it and its pod hurtling through space.

So far, the mission was going according to plan. The body examined the magnetic field of the planet while the mind remembered the coordinates supplied to it by the strategists. Once the Vicious One knew where it was and where the gathering would take place, it headed off.

The Vicious One was not born into a warrior family nor did it have the proper genetics to allow the alchemists to shape it into a warrior. But what it lacked in natural gifts it made up for in grit and determination. As the desert floor raced by underneath its feet, the body recalled the flavor of all the brood members and naysayers and enemies it killed and consumed in its quest to be selected as the leader of a team of scouts.

There was no glory in what the Vicious One did, but its mind told it otherwise. It would be more glory than anyone in its genetic line had ever achieved, and, maybe in some far off future, the species will remember the time when, as extinction loomed, they took this planet and returned to the greatness they lost eons ago. Maybe the elders would ask the Vicious One its secret name, and they would whisper that name to the gods during a spirit quest. Then the Vicious One could live forever.

The mind quickly dismissed the idea. The elders would only ask for the secret names of the warriors that came with the second wave, the ones who would prepare the planet for harvest. A scout's only duty was to make sure the planet was ready for conquest.

The sun passed its zenith before the Vicious One reached the rocky hill where it would meet the rest of its team. The angle of the light hitting the many boulders cast strange shadows across the desert floor, and the Vicious One found a shadow it could hide under while it waited for its team.

The Vicious One had never witnessed the harvest of a planet. In fact, only a few of the most ancient elders were around for the last harvest. The species had become so weak they couldn't even take care of themselves properly. It knew that the harvest of this planet was an act of desperation. When the alchemists came to the planet with the plague, they also brought with them the last remaining gravity drive. The gravity drive was the only way to bring the rest of the species to the planet. If the Vicious One's team could not find the device or if it had been destroyed, it did not matter if the plague eliminated the humans.

The Terrifying One reached the gathering first, followed by the Hateful One. The Golden One and the Wicked One arrived together.

Including itself, that made only five scouts. After waiting until the sun nearly dipped below the horizon, the Vicious One concluded that the other eleven died when their pods impacted the earth. The team spoke to their gods, asking them to spare some time to seek out the souls of the dead. They did not know the dead members' secret names, and their minds feared that it would be difficult for the gods to find the lost souls.

The Vicious One's body checked the magnetic field to find the direction of the largest settlement that existed in the area before the plague. It prepared its team to leave when the Wicked One brought its attention to a creature in the distance.

The creature crawled slowly towards the meeting place, and as it neared, the team could see that it was one of their own. They raced toward it, finding the Pious One near death, one arm broken and several wounds barely healing on its skin. Black blood leaked from cracks in the Pious One's carapace. Its body did not have the energy to heal itself.

The Vicious One knelt down beside its injured team member. 'What has happened to you?' asked the Vicious One. The smell of grief coming off of the Pious One overpowered even the smell of its pain and its blood. The Vicious One's mind prepared itself for the worst.

Haltingly, fighting through the pain, the Pious One spoke. 'I emerged from my pod, and there was a human standing over me. I killed it, but I knew that if there was one human there would be more. I found their settlement.'

The Pious One took a moment to rest. The Vicious One could tell by the shifting mood of its team members that they, like it, suspected what would come next.

'They were waiting for me,' said the Pious One. 'They were a military unit. I could tell by their weaponry and tactics. I killed them all before fleeing. If I had fled, they would have alerted the rest of their kind.'

'There is no need to justify your actions,' said the Vicious One. Behind it, it heard the Hateful One scoff. It paid no heed because its mind was preoccupied with another thought. The plague failed. Humans still inhabited the planet. There would be no harvest.

The Pious One collapsed with exhaustion. The rest of the team stood silently around it, waiting for the Pious One to whisper its secret name before it died.

The Hateful One did not join with the rest of the team. 'We continue with the mission. We summon the warriors and charge into battle at their side. The humans cannot stand up to our might.'

The other team members tensed with anger. It was a sacred moment for the Pious One, and the Hateful One just showed the blasphemy it was famous for. As claws emerged, the Vicious One stepped between its team and the Hateful One.

'We do our duty. We scout out the area and make sure it is safe for the warriors. We do not know the strength of the humans.'

The Hateful One's skin became paler as its blood vessels withdrew deeper into its body where they would be less likely to take damage in a fight. 'You have no faith in the species. The humans know we are here and are already preparing for the battle. We find the gravity drive and call the species now.'

The Vicious One felt the surface of its skin cool. 'If the humans survived the plague, they have known for a long time that we were coming. We've already lost.' It pained the Vicious One to say it, but it knew that was the truth. According to the librarians, the humans were the most advanced civilization they had ever attacked. But millennia had passed since the last harvest, and many did not think that there were enough resources to survive the transit to the next available planet. In only a generation or two, the species would go extinct.

'They survived the plague, but they must be weakened.' The Hateful One tried to entreat the other team members. They kept their minds away from the conversation and let the Vicious One do all their thinking.

'And what if they have weaponized the plague just as we have?' asked the Vicious One.

Doubt crossed the Hateful One's mind for a moment, but it quickly dismissed that. 'The ancient religions were false. The plague cannot harm us. The alchemists have proven it.'

'While sheltered in their cloisters,' said the Vicious One. 'Can we risk exposing the warriors to the plague. What if it awakens the darkness inside of them? Inside of all of us? It is a worse fate than drifting between stars waiting for death.' Its claws glinted in the moonlight. 'We scout and then summon the species.'

A thick stream of drool dripped from between the Hateful One's teeth, and its muscles quivered with anticipation, signs that the body and the mind were losing control. 'You are a coward, Vicious One. And I curse your name.'

The attack came fast, but the Vicious One moved faster. It dodged sideways and dragged its claws, sharp as fire, across the Hateful One's throat. A thick burst of blood broke out from under the skin, and the Hateful One crashed into the ground.

It started to rise into its fighting stance, its body already healing its wound. The Vicious One did not allow time for another attack. It shoved its hand deep into the Hateful One's open throat and yanked out messy strands of muscles and blood vessels. The Hateful One's eyes began to tremble as its mind realized it was dying.

The Vicious One held onto its opponents head and forced its mouth shut. The Hateful One scratched at the Vicious One, but its failing strength could do no harm. With its dying breaths it tried to scream out its secret name, but the Vicious One held the jaw firmly shut. No one would be asking the gods to find the Hateful One's soul.

The Vicious One dropped the dead sack of flesh to the ground. 'We scout. Then we find the gravity drive.'

The rest just bowed their heads in acquiescence.

The Vicious One brought the dead body over to the Pious One. 'Eat and recover your strength,' it said.

Weakness barely allowing it to move, the Pious One looked up at the Vicious One. 'But I did not kill it,' it whispered.

'Then you owe me your life,' responded the Vicious One.

While the Pious One ate, the rest of the team rested to prepare themselves for the next day. The Vicious One remained awake to take a moment to enjoy a sky with an atmosphere for the first time.

# Chapter Three

The woman got to her feet, resting her hands on her knees until she felt steady enough to stand up straight. Michael Davis watched her, feeling more curious than surprised that he had a visitor.

"You're not supposed to be here, are you?" he asked.

She shook her head. "How did you know?"

It's pretty obvious, Davis thought. "No one's supposed to be here," he said. "I don't exist. And neither do my friends."

The woman started looking around the laboratory, but she kept averting her eyes from the zombies in their cells and casting them towards Davis.

"What's your name?" Davis asked.

Davis's voice startled the woman, almost as if she thought it was a zombie sneaking up behind her. Her eyes wavered with stress. "What does it matter?"

Davis sat down on his bunk and stared at the blank wall in front of him, the wall he'd spent the last nine and a half years staring at. His shoulders slumped, and he let out a sigh. "I guess it doesn't matter." But that was a lie and Davis knew it. The woman was the first person he'd seen in a long time that wasn't trying to get a brain biopsy or a marrow sample out of him.

"I'm sorry. My name's Fiona. Dr. Fiona Todd." Davis didn't realize that she was standing at his window until he looked up. Her returned gaze was calm, almost soft. It was not a look Davis expected to see from someone who survived the war. But his experience was limited. Maybe the outside world was different now?

"My name's Michael Davis. Just Davis is fine. What are you here for?"

Dr. Todd hesitated. "Dr. Cheung sent me to get something." She spoke the man's name like he was some kind of saint.

"I haven't seen him for days. Did he forget one of his weapons?"

"One of his weapons? What do you mean?"

Davis held his hands out like the ringmaster in the circus. "Look around. What do you think is happening here?"

Dr. Todd shrank away, probably from the tone in Davis's voice. He regretted the way he spoke. She probably remembered Cheung as the hero of the war. Davis only knew Cheung as the scientist assigned to study him. He examined his hands, and his eyes moved to the scars on his arms. Sometimes he could still feel the pain of teeth sinking into his skin. It was a lot of pain to remember.

"How did you end up here?" asked Dr. Todd. She stepped forward again and placed one hand on the glass that kept Davis from getting out into the world.

"I was captured."

"No. I meant to ask why aren't you one of them?" She pointed in the direction of the zombies without looking at them.

"I don't know."

"Is that why they're experimenting on you?"

Davis shook his head. "I don't have any memories from before the war. Or even when the war started. I don't really even know who I am." I am a prisoner, Davis told himself. In my cell and in my mind.

"Tell me what you do remember," said Dr. Todd.

His earliest memory entered his dreams enough times already. He didn't want to experience them during his waking hours. "It won't help you."

"But maybe it can help you. Maybe I can help you."

Davis wondered what was going on inside of Dr. Todd's head. "You really want to know?"

She nodded.

The pain in Davis's scars started throbbing again. Did his imagination cause the pain? Or was there zombie venom just under the surface, waiting for its moment to attack? Davis unconsciously checked to make sure the glass separating him from Dr. Todd was still in place. Instead, he saw his own reflection. After all the years staring at the thing, Davis still wasn't sure he could trust that person.

He leaned back, resting his shoulders against the wall. He closed his eyes and found himself back in that forest so many years ago.

The cold air bit into Davis's throat and lungs before escaping from his mouth in a thick stream of fog. He slammed himself into a tree and peered around the edges, watching for any hostiles.

The cold air and the tree. It was his first memory. Darkness covered everything before that moment.

Satisfied that the way was clear, Davis waved back towards his comrades. They emerged from their hiding places one by one and leap frogged past Davis. First came Wally, bald and obese, but as strong as King Kong and as fast as a Ferrari. Next was Nicholas, skinny but so tough he could have been a scarecrow made out of steel and bullet proof vests.

These guys were fighters through and through. Some lost spark in his brain told Davis that he would die for them, and they would do the same for him.

A third person emerged from hiding and ran by Davis. Davis looked right into her eyes and saw nothing. It was like looking into the eyes of a robot. And what was her name? Arlene, Aileen? Something like that. Davis thought a moment, somehow remembering that it was Elise.

In that brief moment as Elise ran by, Davis felt nothing. There was no bond of friendship, no common experience that drew them together. She was just there.

Wally signalled, and Davis leap frogged back to the front of the line. He carried a Garand, a good old fashioned M1, and he liked the weight of the rifle in his hands. Sure, it was more cumbersome than a modern arm, but Davis loved seeing the size of the hole it put in a zombie's head.

They continued their descent into the forest, deeper and deeper until the sun had trouble penetrating through the thick canopy. The temperature kept falling, until breathing felt like inhaling frozen acid. Davis knew they had entered Harrison Wolff's territory.

Davis dug up a memory of a memory. Or maybe it was just an impression? Until a few days ago, Wolff was a nuisance. While everyone else did what they could to survive, fighting zombies, scrounging for food and water, Wolff and his men were satisfied just being highway robbers. They'd take people's stuff, make life difficult in the little colonies that sprung up as people tried to bring back normal to the world.

Davis wanted to go after Wolff long ago. But no one wanted to start a war against a band of humans when there was already a war against the undead. So Wolff grew bolder, and his attitude brought in more followers. He grew stronger and more aggressive. He even started killing the people he robbed. And no one wanted to do anything.

And then Wolff and his men wiped out old man Thatcher and his band. They killed all the men and the boys. And all the old women. The rest of the women and the girls, they kidnapped.

There were breeders out there; Davis remembered that. They were optimists and believed that the war would end some day. So they kidnapped women and turned them into repopulation machines. Usually they just turned into zombie buffets.

Breeders sickened Davis, but they were practical in a deranged sort of way. But Wolff was not one of them.

Wolff expected the world to die, wanted it to die. He may have even needed it to die. And while everyone around him suffered in an apocalypse of blood and rotten flesh, Wolff lived his life to the fullest. Free from society and government and their rules and laws, Wolff finally had an opportunity to make his dreams a reality. Davis knew, somehow, that the kidnapped women would not be used to birth children.

Hatred for Wolff burned in Davis's gut. It was the kind of hatred that could only grow when the object of the hatred was once an ally. Or a dear friend.

Davis couldn't remember why he hated Wolff so much. That was all trapped in the dark past. It was just a feeling without any history. But he did know that even after Wolff slaughtered Thatcher's people, no one wanted to go up against Wolff. So now it was just Davis, Wally, Nicholas, and Elise.

As Davis and his group neared Wolff's camp, they slowed their pace. With only four people, they couldn't charge in guns blazing. They just had to hope that they could get close enough to Wolff to put a bullet through his skull. Whatever happened after that was a decision for the fates.

The roars from the camp, though dulled by distance and the forest, sounded like some kind of drunken college party. So far, Davis hadn't seen any guards, which either meant that Wolff had cleared any zombie hordes from the area or the party was too good to miss. Davis hoped it was the latter. Even a dozen feet away from the camp, there were no guards.

Nicholas led the way, slowly creeping across the forest floor like a spider. He reached a point where the ground fell sharply into a dell and peered over the edge. The cheers and hollers from below swelled and quieted down. Whatever was going on down there transfixed Nicholas, and Davis had to chuck a stone at him to draw his attention.

The rock jolted Nicholas out of his stupor, and he signalled the rest of the group to join him at the edge.

There were about a hundred men in the dell, about forty feet below. Outside the circle of people were several trucks, each modified for carrying zombies. The people all surrounded a pit dug out from a dry creek bed. Inside the pit, a giant of a man raised his arms to elicit the cheers of the crowd. He stood almost ankle deep in a soup of blood and dirt created by the dozen or so zombies lying hacked to pieces on the ground. The giant raised his hands up, stretching out all ten fingers. The crowd yelled their approval.

The giant raised his hands again, this time to the one person who mattered. In the bed of a truck, Wolff sat on a crude, wooden throne, elevated above all the lesser people. He held two scantily clad women on a leash, and they stayed silently on their knees at Wolff's side. The giant raised his ten fingers again, and Wolff laughed as if to mock him. He held up five fingers, and the audience booed. The giant turned back to the crowd, urging them to take his side.

Wolff gave in and let the giant have his way. From outside the crowd, zombie handlers brought the undead towards the pit. The crowd separated faster than oil and water to let the handlers through, and one by one, they threw ten zombies into the pit. The giant raised a fireman's ax from out of the slop at his feet, and the crowd went silent.

"Now's your chance," Wally whispered.

Davis nodded. Some part of him was actually curious to know if the giant could handle the ten zombies, but he was still more interested to know what Wolff's brains would look like splattered on the ground.

He brought his rifle to his shoulder and rested it on a fallen branch for stability. He adjusted his sights and lined them up with Wolff's face. The man slouched in his throne, not moving much, giving Davis an easy shot.

Davis slowed his breathing, ignoring the burn of the icy air. He controlled his nerves and prepared for the shot. Off to his left, he heard a faint rustle. The sound of feet moving through dead leaves.

Instinct forced him to roll to his side. In a single instant, Davis saw Elise's eyes still staring into the battle arena and one of Wolff's men sneaking up behind her, and he heard the crack of his own rifle as he sent a bullet ripping through the man's chest. The man was dead before his heart could explode out of his back, and Wally and Nicholas fired wildly into the crowd, hoping to hit Wolff.

Everyone below either scattered or fired their weapons at the attackers above. The gunfire distracted the giant, and he went down under the claws and hungry bites of the zombie gladiators.

Wolff's followers jumped up to shield their leader, and whenever one of them went down, another would take his place. Some of the men tried to scramble up the escarpment to get to Davis and his group. They would have been easy pickings, but there was only so much ammunition to go around, and the mission was a failure.

"Retreat!" Davis yelled. Elise grabbed him by the shoulder. He couldn't remember if she said anything or if there was any expression on her face. "Run!" he yelled to his group.

They each fired a few more futile shots at Wolff before breaking off and charging into the forest and away from Wolff's territory.

They didn't get far. Several trucks drove up and surrounded them. Wolff's men jumped out and raised their weapons at Davis and his people. Outnumbered and outgunned, Davis ordered Wally, Nicholas, and Elise to drop their guns.

Each of the trucks was modified so that the entire bed became a giant metal box. The door on the back of each box was held shut by a heavy bolt. Inside, Davis heard scratching and snarls. The trucks belonged to the zombie handlers.

A few minutes later, another truck drove up. The throne on the back was empty, but Wolff still looked the part of a medieval warlord sitting in the driver's seat. He got out and approached Davis, ignoring the others.

Wolff had the happy expression of a man who just ate a big steak dinner, not that of someone who just survived an assassination. "You should have just stayed home, Davis. Now the rest of your people will have to suffer for your transgressions."

Davis raised his fist and lunged at Wolff. With less effort than it would have taken to scratch his ass, Wolff smashed his elbow into Davis's nose and swatted him to the ground. Davis landed next to his rifle. As he reached for it, Wolff drove his booted foot deep into Davis's gut.

"You go to hell," Davis growled when his air returned.

"This is hell," Wolff said, holding his hands out to the world around him. "It is the most beautiful place I have ever seen."

As he headed back to his truck, Wolff motioned to the zombie handlers, and they opened the boxes on their trucks. The handlers cattleprodded the zombies out of the trucks, urging them to form a circle around the failed assassins. Wally dove for his gun. In one motion, Wolff turned around, drew his revolver, and put a bullet through Wally's knee. The force of the blast nearly took off the man's leg, but a few loose tendons kept it attached to the rest of his body. Nicholas jumped to Wally's side. Wally was in too much pain to scream or cry, but the look on his friend's face drove Nicholas over the edge. He reached for Wally's gun, and Wolff sent a bullet to shatter Nicholas's hand.

The scent of blood and the crack of gunfire drove the zombies crazy. Their jaws chomped at air just to get a tiny taste of blood.

Wolff blew the smoke out of the barrel of his gun and holstered it with a flourish. "Anyone else?" he asked. He gave Davis and Elise his most devilish smile and got into his truck.

With a desperate dive, Davis snatched up his rifle and pointed it at Wolff. Without aiming, he fired a shot. The bullet tore the skin from Wolff's face, leaving a mess of shredded flesh and broken bone. A scream, as terrifying and painful as that of a dying animal, escaped from what once was Wolff's mouth. One of his men pushed the leader aside to take the driver's seat and drove off into the woods.

The zombie handlers had no idea what to do, so they just shoved the zombies at their enemies. The freshest blood leaked out of Nicholas and Wally, and the zombies knew they were the easiest prey. Davis fired off a few rounds at the handlers, hitting two of them. They served as a distraction to some of the zombies and gave Nicholas and Wally a little breathing room.

While Elise shot at any approaching zombies, Davis helped Nicholas drag Wally towards one of the handler's trucks, blasting any zombie that got too close in the face. Blood flowed freely from Nicholas's stump of a wrist, and sweat poured over his increasingly wan face.

A couple of zombies feasted on a handler within feet of the truck's door. The keys glinted in the handler's dead hand. Davis shot one zombie in the face, and his rifle pinged as it ran out of ammo. He flipped the gun around and brought the butt down on the other zombie's head, collapsing its skull into its chest. For good measure, he stomped the handler's head into mush, saving him from his eventual fate.

Nicholas retrieved the keys and swung the truck's door open. A zombie, fresh gore dripping from its wide open maw, surged out of the vehicle. Its teeth sank deep into Nicholas's throat, taking a large mouthful, then swung its head back, stretching and snapping Nicholas's skin, muscles, and arteries. Hot blood bathed the zombie's face, and it drank before going in for more meat.

Davis only realized this too late. He clubbed the zombie with his rifle and cracked its skull open. Nicholas squirmed on the ground, using his hand and his stump to try to stop the flow of blood. Within seconds he was dead.

A scream prevented Davis from saving Nicholas from returning from the dead. Elise tripped over a rock, and her rifle went sailing out of her reach. A clawed hand stabbed through her pants and into her leg, pulling away strands of cloth and flesh. She kicked at the undead attackers, but more hands reached for her.

Club held high, Davis stormed into battle. Zombies fell under his assault, and Elise took the opportunity to retrieve her rifle and retreat. For the first time, Davis saw just how many zombies Wolff owned. Too many. And for the first time in the battle, Davis felt his heart pump so fast he wanted to puke.

A swift kick sent one zombie flying towards the others, and Davis used the distraction to glance around. Elise was a safe distance away, but she still watched the battle. Davis stepped back and prepared to run towards her, but he stumbled over Wally's bulk.

In his panic, he had forgotten his friend, and Davis swore at himself. He tried to lift Wally up, but the man was just too heavy.

"No!" Elise screamed.

Davis glanced at her, and in that moment he felt teeth dig into his shoulder. He pushed that zombie away, but the next one was already upon him. He held his arm up, sacrificing it to save his throat. Under the weight of the zombie, he collapsed, and four more went in for the kill. The rest went for Wally and peeled open his abdomen to get to his organs.

Teeth and claws rent his flesh, and the blood flowing over his face burned his eyes. Through a haze of red he saw Elise's face. Was she scared? Was she sad? Davis couldn't remember. All she did was stand there, watching him get eaten alive. Any hint of her mental state hid behind the fog of lost memories.

Davis spoke and choked on his blood. He tried again and "help me" gargled out of his throat. The code words for "kill me."

Elise heard him. She twitched and looked down at him. Then she took one step back. Then another. Then she ran away into the forest.

Rage boiled through his bloody and ruined muscles. Davis almost felt himself smile. The only thing he could do now was fight.

# CHAPTER FOUR

Fiona let Davis sit in silence for a few moments. She wondered how much of what he said was true, and how much was just his mind making up a story he could believe in. The way his eyes fluttered behind the lids and the calmness of his voice made Fiona think that Davis narrated a dream, not a memory. The trauma of surviving a zombie attack could have affected his mind.

"What happened next?" she asked when she thought she had given him enough time.

Davis opened his eyes and shrugged, as if the answer was not that important. "I killed them all."

"Did you go after this Elise person?" During the war, revenge killings happened all the time. When life revolved around being stronger and smarter than everyone else, a person did what they had to stay on top. Fiona unconsciously shook her head to clear out those thoughts.

Davis continued. "No. I was too sick. I didn't have enough energy to kill myself, so I just waited and waited to turn into one of those things." He pointed outside his chamber at one of the lab's captive zombies. Fiona looked even if she didn't want to. "It was the worst pain I'd ever felt," he continued. "Worse than almost getting hacked to pieces by the zombies. It was like food poisoning. But with more blood and less control. Then all the bites got infected. Leaking pus everywhere. I must have looked like a wax statue in the sun."

Davis laughed, and Fiona laughed, too, even if the thought of it turned her stomach. "How did you survive?"

"No idea. My memory started going when I was sick. The first thing I remember is all that stuff I just told you. Hunting Wolff. The forest. Hell, I don't even know where that forest is. Sometimes I get these feelings, like I'm going to remember what life was like before, but nothing happens."

"How'd you end up here?"

Davis gave another shrug. "One moment I thought I was dying, the next I wake up in the back of an RV. An old couple found me. Fixed me up. We fought and killed together for a while. Beatrice got lucky and died of a heart attack. Jack killed himself a few weeks later. I made it through the war. Tried to make a new life. It wasn't even half a year before they found me and put me in here."

Fiona shuddered slightly. He was a test subject, a prisoner, for ten years now. While everyone else started rebuilding, Davis woke up every morning to the sounds of mad zombies. Stuck in a cell, surrounded by the horrors of the past, with only his memories for company. He was a true prisoner.

Davis stood up and leaned his back against the glass, facing away from Fiona. "Do you ever wonder what happened to people you knew? Friends you hadn't seen in years? Maybe family on the other side of the country?"

Fiona thought of the refugee city, wondering again if her parents were trapped in one somewhere. "Yes, of course. Everyone does."

"I don't. I have no memory of any friends or family. Maybe I've always been alone in this world." Davis turned around and slammed his fists into the glass. He stared at Fiona with eyes like obsidian, their cold darkness hiding the fire that once burned inside. "That's the real torture. Not this." He waved around at his prison cell.

The zombies' cries and growls grew more agitated. Fiona tried to block it out, but her gut knotted at the familiar sound. The sound of feeding time. It was torture to her.

"Do you remember your first kill?" Davis asked.

Mrs. Gibson. Fiona didn't even know she had turned until it was almost too late. She smashed the zombie's head in with a shovel and proceeded to destroy the rest of the body until someone stopped her. "Yes."

"What did it feel like?"

"It was scary. I didn't want to do it. I thought I was killing a person, not a zombie." Fiona shifted uncomfortably.

"But the second was easier?"

"And it got easier the more I killed," Fiona said, surprising herself with her defensiveness.

Davis chuckled, though Fiona couldn't hear it over the ever louder zombies. "I don't remember my first kill. I just remember the part about it being easy. Even when I shot Wolff or any of his followers, I didn't think I was shooting other human beings. I was just getting rid of the garbage. It makes me wonder if I ever had a hard time killing. Was it always so easy?"

Fiona didn't know how to respond. She had said the killing got easier. That didn't mean killing wasn't difficult.

"You better get on with your mission," said Davis. "It's almost feeding time."

The zombies were in a near frenzy. Fiona almost found it amusing that the zombies had a Pavlovian reaction to their feeding, but the thought of feeding zombies sickened her. "What do they eat?" she asked meekly.

"Pork," said Davis with a smile. "With maybe a little seasoning from the blood bank. I just get regular hospital food."

Fiona tried to laugh. "How do we get you out of here?"

"We don't. You do. Just find your thing and get out. You've wasted enough time with me."

"No. This isn't right."

Davis shrugged. "You can't do anything about it. Just find whatever it is you're looking for."

Fiona pulled out her ID card. There was a card reader next to Davis's cell, and Fiona swiped the card. The light indicator on the reader flashed red. Fiona swiped again with the same result.

"There aren't too many people with the authorization to open this cell," said Davis. "That card won't work."

"I know," snapped Fiona. She tried to make eye contact with Davis but couldn't. He seemed calm, as if he didn't care if he could get out of his cell. Fiona felt ashamed that she couldn't help him.

She knew that she should just leave it be, should just find Dr. Cheung's vial, but there was something about Davis that made her think that getting him out of his cell was the right thing to do. It was for the same reason that she wanted to help Dr. Cheung. She needed to do it for herself.

Fiona swiped the card one last time.

"I'm sorry," said Davis. Fiona stepped back. That was what she wanted to say.

She nodded in response. "I have to look for something," she mumbled and walked away. For the second time that day, she found herself cursing her choices. But was it really a choice? As a survivor of the war, did she have a duty to try to make the world a better place? She didn't know, but for the past ten years it felt like she had done nothing.

There were dozens, maybe hundreds of containers of different chemicals and solutions in the lab. It hurt Fiona's eyes just trying to read the labels on all of them. And the zombies' incessant growlings didn't help her concentration either.

"Hey! Hey!" Davis yelled.

Fiona whirled around. Davis simply stood and pointed in the direction of the elevator. The light above it was illuminated. Someone was about to enter the lab.

"Find somewhere to hide," said Davis.

There weren't many good hiding places in the lab, but Fiona crammed herself in the space between two large machines just before the elevator doors opened.

Fiona peeked between her machines to get a look. Three men stepped out. One was a huge guy, possibly an orderly. He stayed behind the other two and looked like he was waiting for his orders. The other two were military.

The subordinate put on a mean face, as if he were trying to be more intimidating than he really was. He only succeeded in looking weak and too eager to please. He wore his uniform not for the pride of wearing the uniform, but for the superiority it gave him over others.

The other one had a confident stride that separated him from his companion, or any ordinary man for that matter. He stood tall, and wrinkles formed by time and stress lined his face. His prime years most certainly passed him a long time ago, but Fiona would not have been surprised if the man could have wrestled a tiger and won.

"General Wilcox," said Davis. "What brings you and Hop-Frog down here?"

The subordinate man stepped forward, puffing up his chest and baring his teeth. "You're lucky I'm not in there with you."

Wilcox stopped the other man. "Halley, calm down."

Halley shrunk away. "Yes, sir."

"Where is she?" asked Wilcox. Fiona tried to make herself smaller in her hiding place. That guard up in the hospital was suspicious after all.

"I don't know what you're talking about," said Davis. He leaned against the glass partition and scratched his chin as casually as possible. Halley pulled his pistol and started poking his head into every possible hiding spot while Davis and Wilcox kept talking.

The elevator door was still open. Fiona just had to wait for the Halley guy to look the wrong way. The orderly didn't look that fast. She could make it to the elevator before she got caught. Halley got closer. Fiona wondered one last time why she thought she had to help Davis.

Then she bolted for the elevator. Over the pounding of her footsteps, she heard both Davis and Halley curse. Halley started shooting, and Fiona crouched down to make herself a smaller target. The bullets crashed into one of the zombie's cells, creating a web-like pattern of cracked glass.

"Halley, you idiot!" yelled Wilcox.

The orderly tried to grab Fiona, and while she ducked out of the reach of his arms, her feet bumped into his extended leg. Her outstretched hands stopped her from breaking her nose on the floor, but the orderly's big hand around her ankle told her that she'd been caught.

Glass shattered and cascaded across the floor as a zombie broke free from its cell, its cries no longer muted by the glass. It went for the orderly, grabbing him from behind and forcing its bony fingers into his mouth. It pulled back on the man's cheeks, removing the skin like a mask.

The orderly scrambled away, screaming and sobbing. And Fiona became the zombie's nearest target. She started backing away towards the elevator, but the zombie, motivated by hunger, moved faster than she thought its rotting body could possibly move.

"Hey! Stop right there!" It was Davis. And for some reason, the zombie obeyed him. It stood still and dropped the pieces of cheeks from its hands.

Fiona's mind raced. It shouldn't have been possible. Zombies didn't have any intelligence. Only instinct. They didn't listen to orders. Was it really Davis? Was this a result of his attack?

Wilcox drew a pistol and put it against the zombie's temple before pulling the trigger.

Fiona closed her eyes, and when she opened them again, Halley stood over her. He held a syringe in one hand, and he bent over and shoved the needle into Fiona's neck.

# CHAPTER FIVE

Major Thomas Halley pulled the needle out of the woman's neck. "She'll be out for a while," he said.

General Wilcox stood over the both of them and examined the woman. "She probably works for Cheung. Are you sure that she'll be out?"

"Yes, sir. This dose is big enough to take out Davis."

"Then are you sure you didn't kill her?"

Halley hadn't really thought about it. All he knew was that they needed her alive and that the tranquilizer always worked on Davis. He never bothered or cared to ask Cheung about appropriate dosing before. "I think she'll be all right."

"She better be. We need to find Cheung." The general walked away and headed towards Davis's cell. "And take care of that orderly."

The man lay passed out on the ground. The white of his teeth showed through in the places where the zombie ripped his cheeks off. A steady trickle of blood pumped out of the busted arteries in his face, indicating he still lived. "I don't think he's been bitten," said Halley. "He won't be pretty but he'll live."

"I don't care," said Wilcox. "We can't risk him turning."

"Maybe we should wait."

"Just do it." The tone of Wilcox's voice didn't change, but the menace in his eyes could have stabbed Halley through the heart.

"Yes, sir." Halley refilled his syringe. He didn't know anything about dosing, but he knew that the massive dose he gave to the orderly would be lethal.

Wilcox waited for a few moments to make sure Halley did what he was told. Then he turned to Davis.

The prisoner sat on his bunk, trying his best to look like he didn't care about the goings on outside of his cell. But Halley had spent enough time with Davis to know that it was all a ruse. The woman was probably the first person he had seen since his capture that didn't work for Wilcox. She was certainly the first female he had seen since then, not counting the zombies.

"Did she say what she was looking for?" asked Wilcox.

"We didn't really talk much," said Davis. "People don't tend to trust prisoners."

"Did she mention Dr. Cheung?"

"We didn't really talk."

"What was she doing down here?"

"I don't know. Maybe she got lost?"

Wilcox waved his hand through the air as if he were trying to brush away Davis's words.

Halley stepped forward. "We can gas him, sir. Then we can tie him up and interrogate him properly."

The general didn't respond. He seemed to be deep in thought. He paced around the room for a while then went to a shelf where Cheung kept his various chemicals or whatever. Halley never really asked what all of those things were for. Wilcox played around with some of the glass containers, and that seemed to satisfy him.

"We'll wait for the girl to wake up," said Wilcox. "We'll ask her then." He got into the elevator. When Halley didn't follow, he gave the major an annoyed glance. Halley rushed to join him.

They rode back up to the hospital in silence and walked back to their office building without exchanging any words. It would have been an awkward moment for anybody else, but Halley knew that Wilcox's silence meant that he was doing his job right. Burglars and dead orderlies be damned. As long as Halley kept on Wilcox's good side, everything was good.

The general checked his watch, and instead of heading to Wilcox's office, they went into the empty boardroom.

"Is your gun loaded?" asked Wilcox.

"I'm down a few rounds, sir. From back in the lab."

"Put in a fresh magazine. And keep your gun loose in the holster. We have a business meeting."

Halley obeyed, and Wilcox made sure his gun was all right. He didn't sit at the head of the table like he usually did. Instead, he sat on the side so that whoever his visitor was would have to sit and face him, and Halley could stand behind the visitor. If the visitor tried anything funny, they would get caught between Halley's and Wilcox's crossfire.

They waited in silence for a few minutes, and then Wilcox nodded to Halley. Over the intercom, Halley asked the general's secretary to send in their visitor.

She walked in alone, wearing a black cloak, hood up and front closed. The shadows cast by the hood did nothing to hide the paleness of her face. She reminded Halley of those goth kids he used to make fun of back in high school, years before the war. But she wasn't an angsty teenager. She was something else. To Halley, just being in her presence felt dangerous. It was like coming face to face with a mad cobra.

She'd been in to see the general a few times before, but Halley had never been asked to stand guard before. He racked his mind to remember her name.

Elise. He was pretty sure that was it.

She took the seat across from Wilcox. Halley stood behind her and just off to the side. If the general had to shoot, Halley didn't want any bullets passing through Elise and into him.

Elise spoke first. "I'm very busy. What is it that you want?" If snakes could talk, that's what their voice would sound like, thought Halley. Inhuman.

Wilcox leaned back in his chair. He kept one hand on the table, but the other was in his lap, inches away from his holster. "A naval vessel pulled into the port of Long Beach today. My understanding is that your people were at the helm."

"Yes, it belongs to us."

"And why is that? We agreed that I would be in charge of all military affairs."

"And we agreed many years ago that you would eliminate Dr. Robert Cheung. I hear he has gone missing."

Halley tensed up. Cheung's involvement with Wilcox was purely voluntary, but his existence was just as much a secret as Davis's. What did Elise know? What was Wilcox involved in?

The general's face barely betrayed any emotion, but Halley recognized a little tick at the corner of Wilcox's mouth that indicated he was hiding something. "Cheung had uses. Eliminating him would have made it more difficult to deal with our . . . future problems."

"And has he proven useful?" asked Elise. She sounded amused by Wilcox's excuse.

Wilcox nodded. "He has. And if you want him eliminated, it'll be done. Now, about your war ship."

"We need it to deal with our future problems."

"That's fair enough. I just hope you're not planning anything behind my back." The general's mouth twitched again.

"Of course we aren't," said Elise. Her voice sounded more inhuman to Halley's ears then ever before. "Did you see the meteor shower the other night?"

The sudden change in direction for the conversation threw Wilcox off guard. "What do you mean?"

"I asked if you had seen it."

"I saw some of it. Why?"

"Our future problem is no longer in the future. I sent several men to test out the problem, but they were all eliminated. I wanted to give you fair warning."

Wilcox's eyes widened with shock, and when he calmed down, a deadly smile spread across his lips.

Halley had seen that smile hundreds of times before. But the last time he saw it was during the war. It was the smile Wilcox always had when the only hope of surviving against a horde of zombies was to kill them all. Halley imagined it was the same smile Jack the Ripper's victims saw before they died. In his own way, Wilcox was just as inhuman as Elise.

Elise stood up and headed for the exit. "I'll be returning to the city. Events may prove hectic in the near future. I'll send some of my servants to work with you."

Wilcox got up from his chair. His hand still stayed close to his pistol. "Just to update you, as we may be out of contact for a while, my people still haven't found the object."

Elise turned around. Her eyes shone bright, even under the shadow of her hood. "I believe you."

She left, and Wilcox took his usual seat at the head of the table. Halley stood patiently at his side. Halley wondered why Wilcox finally decided to let him sit in on his conversation with Elise. He knew that the general was hiding something from her. But what? But mostly, Halley felt a soft pain in his heart. Why didn't Wilcox trust him until now?

After a minute or two, Wilcox took a cell phone out of his pocket. It was some kind of monstrosity. Halley had seen it a few times and figured it was designed for security.

Wilcox dialed a number and waited for the other line to pick up. "Mr. Rex? Yes, it's me . . . It's time . . . All of them. And all of your guns . . . I think it will be very violent. Thank you." The general hung up.

"Sir, if I may ask?" said Halley.

Wilcox grunted in response.

"What's happening?"

For a moment, Wilcox remained silent, as if he were deciding if it was wise to tell Halley anything. Halley had a feeling that this silence did not mean that he was doing the right thing.

"I apologize for intruding, sir."

"Aliens, Major. It's an invasion."

A little chuckle escaped Halley's lips accidentally. "Aliens?"

"That's exactly what I said." Wilcox got up, and Halley followed him to his office.

Halley knew the general had said "aliens," but the word just had no meaning to him. He could believe in a zombie war; he lived through one. But aliens? It sounded too weird to be true.

Wilcox took a giant syringe out of the safe he kept behind his desk. The size of the needle made Halley think it was some kind of medieval torture device.

"We need to find Cheung," said Wilcox. "I suspect that he may have something that will give me an advantage over Elise and her people. I don't think that she has my best interests in mind. I don't trust her, and I think that she doesn't trust me." He handed the syringe to Halley.

"What is this for?" asked Halley.

"The girl. The one in the lab. It'll wake her up. Find out what she knows about Cheung. Torture her if you must. Make sure Davis sees it. Maybe he'll talk, too."

Halley didn't particularly like torture, but he was good at it. And the general had given him an order, and good soldiers always obeyed their orders.

# CHAPTER SIX

Knowing that there were humans on the planet, finding them became easy enough. Early scouts reported that humans were primitive, but they were not without technology. The body could just barely feel the movement of electricity used as power, and following the trail led the team to a settlement.

The Vicious One knew to expect a lot of humans, but upon seeing the massive collection of them, the mind started to shut down. The plague did not do its job of eliminating the threat of intelligent life forms on the planet, and now the chances of successfully harvesting the planet plummeted. The body released a stimulating chemical that kept the Vicious One's mind aware.

'It appears to be some kind of prison,' said the Golden One. Its clawed hand pointed out the walls and various towers surrounding the gathering of humans. If it was a prison, the towers would have allowed the guards to watch over the inmates.

'It is not like any prison I have seen,' said the Wicked One. 'It is too chaotic. Look how the humans inside have created dwellings of their own. And that area there looks as if it is set up for merchants to do business.'

The Vicious One peered down from its team's vantage point high above the supposed prison, observing the features that the Golden One and the Wicked One noted. The prison was built against the side of a hill, human-built walls forming the front of the prison and a cliff-face carved from the hill making the last wall. The team perched on top of the hill, and at the top, far above the other three walls, and under cover of night, they could watch the humans without fear of being seen.

'Perhaps,' suggested the Vicious One, 'they keep the infected humans in there to protect the uninfected.'

'Why not eliminate them?' asked the Pious One. Its wounds were nearly healed, thanks to the nutrients from the Hateful One's body.

None suggested an answer. If the plague still existed on the planet, it would completely eliminate the planet's potential as a resource. The Vicious One's mind and body experienced a simultaneous wave of despair.

According to the scholars, there was a time when the species could have simply avoided the planet. Their technology let them harvest the uninhabited planets. But over time and through the deterioration of society, that technology was lost. In this solar system, the heavy gravity and hurricane winds of the gas giants would destroy any vessel in seconds. The extremes of temperatures on the other planets were too much even for the most adaptive of bodies. In this system, only the third planet from the sun was suitable for harvest, but a sophisticated and weaponized life form inhabited it.

The Vicious One detected a scent that suggested the others were feeling the same desperation as it felt. It turned to face the rest of its team. 'I know the species is nearing its end. And the presence of the humans may be what finally dooms us. But we do not have all the information yet. We are scouts. We will perform our duty, even if it is futile. Maybe we can find some source of hope. We continue with our mission. When we have learned all that we could, we find the gravity drive.'

The smell of the team's anguish faded into the night, but it did not disappear.

'How do we start?' asked the Pious One.

'We split up,' said the Vicious One. 'I do not see an encampment for the guards, if this is a prison. There must be another place where the guards dwell, and there must be a local economy supporting them. And if there are more dwellings, there must be some form of agriculture in the area.'

The Vicious One assigned his team different areas to explore, with the instructions that they return to their spot on the top of the cliff after four days. For its own assignment, the Vicious One decided that it wanted to explore the prison.

The team went their separate ways, and the Vicious One crawled down the cliff. The cliff face was nearly perpendicular to the ground, but the Vicious One's claws sank easily into the rock, making the climb simple. The earliest scouting reports, created long before the plague was released, suggested that humans did not have the ability to climb such a cliff without special equipment. And if the prisoners were to try, the guards could catch them easily. But the guards would be trained to find those climbing out of the prison. They did not suspect that the Vicious One would climb into it. Despite its bulk, the Vicious One moved smoothly and silently.

It crept across the rooftops, staying in the shadows when it could, its body adjusting its color when it could not. It picked its steps carefully, trying not to break the dwellings that seemed to be made from cast-off materials. It sensed that too much motion would result in the buildings' weak joints failing.

The Vicious One could not be sure, but it observed that night time was the human's time for rest and leisure. It peered through windows, watching humans sleep or socialize. It couldn't read their body language, but none looked to be infected.

The body perceived an array of new smells, some of them pleasant, some noxious. The mind blocked out the most intense smells and sorted through the different scents to determine the chemical compositions. The scent of rotting meat interested the Vicious One the most. After investigation, the source often turned out to be some non-human animal, long dead and forgotten in the street. One time, it actually was a human, buried under piles of waste in an alley. The human had several stab wounds in its midsection. Though the human reeked of decay, the Vicious One did not smell any infection in it.

Its investigation lasted through the night, and the sun just started to lighten the horizon when the Vicious One decided that it needed to hide. It was confident in its ability to evade detection even in the light of day, but its mind decided that hiding would be the best option. It found many abandoned buildings during the night, and it picked one to spend the day in. If any human were to find it, the Vicious One thought that it would be easy enough to kill and no one would miss it. They left one of their own to rot in an alley, after all.

It found a suitable spot to wait out the day when it picked up a new scent. At first, it thought that it was the plague, a scent that its mind and body had been forced to memorize long before the mission started. It was similar, but different in such a way that the mind had to filter out the growing sense of fear in the Vicious One's body.

The infection burned like ammonia and coated the scent organs with a fetid mixture of decay and pain. But the air assaulting the Vicious One now was nothing like that. It was more powerful, as if the infection was just a diluted sample of it. Its mind and its body could not block the scent, and the Vicious One found itself surrounded by a miasma of pure corruption.

In the building's bottom layers, the Vicious One heard dozens of footfalls, and they grew louder as they ascended the building. Several humans entered into the Vicious One's room. They moved efficiently and as one, a trained team. They carried metal objects in their hands that the Vicious One could only assume were the weapons the Pious One encountered back in the desert city. Each of them carried the corruption within them, but not enough to be the source of the foul fragrance.

Before they could take up their positions, the Vicious One attacked. It dashed forward, demolishing one human with its claws. The others fired their weapons towards the spot where their teammate's blood still filled the air, but the Vicious One had already moved on to its next victim. It grabbed the human by the leg and swung it like a flail at another. Their skeleton's shattered with a sound like the splitting of stone. The human in the Vicious One's hand still lived, as evidenced by its efforts to move its broken limbs and the fountains of blood that drowned out its attempted cries. The Vicious One flung it at another human, and they both crashed through a window and down to the streets below.

A human opened fire, and the Vicious One felt the bite of small projectiles entering its skin. The weapons the humans carried were indeed some kind of gun, and they used some kind of bullet as ammunition. The Vicious One's body shifted organs and blood vessels to minimize damage, and it sent cells to start closing the wounds. Even in the middle of the fight, the Vicious One's mind felt amusement at the human's choice of weaponry. Guns were only used by fragile species that could not stand in face-to-face combat.

The Vicious One drove its claws into the human's gut and lifted it off the floor, using all of its strength to open the human's skull against the ceiling. The remaining humans shot the Vicious One in the back, but its carapace deflected the bullets. It pounced on them, showing them claws and teeth that cut like the sun.

Mere moments later, the Vicious One stood in a pile of ruined humans, their blood flooding the floor and pouring through the cracks into the room below. Some of the humans still lived, but the damage on their bodies was impossible to heal, even if humans could heal themselves.

The Vicious One's body started to recuperate, breaking down the bullets to use them as energy. Its mind started to decide what to do next when the odor of corruption came again. It assaulted the senses with the force of a meteor, so strong was its scent in the Vicious One's mind.

Another human entered, flanked by several more like the ones just defeated. This one was different. It did not carry the weapons of a warrior, nor did it have the same dress as the others. It had long black hair, and the paleness of its skin suggested sickness, but it carried itself with strength and poise. Its build was different than its underlings, slighter and more graceful. The Vicious One remembered that humans displayed sexual dimorphism, and it thought that this new human was a female.

Without a doubt, she was the warriors' leader. But more importantly, she was the source of the corruption.

The Vicious One's mind and body froze, even if they knew it must escape.

A warrior went up to the leader's side, holding an object draped in cloth. The woman pulled the cloth aside, revealing the head of a scholar, a member of the Vicious One's species. The head smelled ancient, but through some unknown alchemy the skin on the head kept trying to heal itself, even if it should have been long dead. The extra skin sloughed off and splattered on the ground before a new cycle of skin growth began. The eyes were clouded with death, but they twitched and spun independently of each other. A plastic tube inserted into the brain cavity connected to a device on the warrior's back. From the device, some kind of fluid pumped into the head, presumably nutrients to extend the scholar's unnatural life.

The small size and delicate features identified the skull as that of a scholar, but the misshapen bone growths and deformities suggested some kind of inbred disease. It was a member of the Vicious One's species, but it was not one of them. It was one of the Others. The Vicious One's mind and body felt a strange emotion that it had never experienced before. The Others were thought dead millennia ago, and here was one on the planet that the species intended to harvest. It was worse than if the plague still lived.

The Vicious One bared its claws and prepared for the most important fight of its life. Then it heard its secret name.

The sound did not have a direction. It came from all around, echoing through physical and mental space. The secret name repeated over and over until the Vicious One identified the source. It came from the head.

Hearing its secret name, which no one but itself knew, weakened the Vicious One. It slumped to the floor, and the warriors rushed in to bind it. The Vicious One did not struggle, but it would have proven futile anyway. The bonds were not created by humans. They used technology known only to its species.

The woman replaced the cloth on the scholar's head just as it sent a shock of pain into the Vicious One's mind. The mind went dark, and the body became numb.

# Chapter Seven

An intense pain shot through Fiona's shoulder. She thought that a zombie had finally gotten her, that its saliva was soaking into her flesh. She was done. If she didn't move, she'd get eaten piece by piece. But if she ran, she'd slowly join the undead. She would suffer for days until, finally, every last bit of her humanity died, only to be replaced with a never-ending hunger.

Her eyes fluttered open to meet a cold stare. What was his name? Halley? She thought that was right. The pain in her shoulder lessened as Halley pulled a gigantic needle out of it. He smiled at her.

"I'm sorry, but I'm going to have to torture you," said Halley. "I don't want to, but I will."

Even with her grogginess, Fiona wasn't convinced. It was more like Halley was trying to reassure himself than Fiona, telling a lie that he wanted to believe.

"You leave her alone!" yelled Davis. "Touch her, and I will break you."

Halley rushed over to Davis's cell and slammed his hand against the glass. "How? You're just an animal in a cage."

The muscles in Davis's jaw worked as he tried to control his anger.

While the two men stared each other down, Fiona realized that she had a great opportunity to escape. She didn't feel any ropes around her wrists or ankles, so she was free to just get up and go. With more effort than it should have taken, she got to her feet and lost control.

Her knees wobbled, and the world started spinning. Gravity pulled her backwards, and she crashed into a table full of lab instruments. Glass shattered on the ground, and all Fiona could do was lay in the mess and wait for her strength to return.

Halley cursed and dragged a chair over by Fiona. He picked her up and set her down hard on the chair. "Don't do anything stupid," he said. "I have orders to torture you. Not kill you." He brought the table back to standing and walked around her. She heard him rummaging through something, and then he set his tools down on the table.

He had pepper spray, a handheld taser, a staple gun, a hammer, and various dental tools. He laid each down with care, making sure that Fiona got a good look at all of them. She wanted to cry or puke or scream or die. She didn't know which. She just knew that the sickness she felt in her gut and the imagined pain her brain anticipated would be nothing compared to what was about to come.

"I usually start small," said Halley. "The things that hurt but won't really cause any permanent damage. It gives you an experience of pain, but you know it's only temporary. It gives you a chance to tell me what I want to know before we move on to the next stage. When we get to a tool like the hammer, you'll definitely talk. Because with each whack, you'll know that's one finger or toe you'll never get back. And if that doesn't work, just remember that we're in a laboratory. I don't know much about chemistry, but I know what 'acid' means. It means pain and disfigurement. When I'm done, you won't want to ever see yourself in a mirror."

Halley stood and hitched up his pants. Davis pressed his hands against the glass. He had the sad look of someone who knew they were helpless. Fiona's heart beat so fast it became a constant hum instead of a pulse. Sweat flowed down her face, and she wanted to beg, but her mind wouldn't work.

"Now, knowing all that," said Halley, "will you tell me where Dr. Cheung is?"

Fiona's jaw moved up and down, but no words came out. Halley grinned.

He grabbed the pepper spray and held it close to Fiona's face. With his free hand, he pulled her eyelids wide open. The nozzle of the pepper spray was only an inch away, and Fiona tried to knock Halley's arm away, but she was still too weak.

Halley stood up and laughed. "No, it's too early for that." He traded the pepper spray for the taser, and without any flourish or announcement, he jammed the device into Fiona's gut.

The sharp crackle of electricity boomed like a gunshot in the laboratory, and the zombies started howling, as if they could taste pain in the air. Fiona's back arched, and the force of her muscle spasms threw her out of her chair. She landed face first in the broken glass on the ground. Halley hit her a few more times in the ribs.

Davis's yelling and cursing was incomprehensible over the zombies' cries and Halley's cackling. Fiona thought her face was bleeding, but it was only hot tears pouring down her face. She blinked to clear her eyes, and the gigantic needle was right in front of her.

Halley grabbed the back her collar to drag her to her feet. Fiona swung her arm and jabbed the syringe towards his face. The thick metal needle stuck itself in Halley's jaw and snapped off. He tried to pull the thing out of his face and dropped the taser.

Fiona grabbed it before he realized his mistake and shocked him in the leg. He collapsed to the ground, his seizures so intense his hands pulled the needle out of his jaw. Fiona kept it going until foam started pouring out of Halley's mouth.

She tossed the taser aside and looked up at Davis. He seemed impressed. "We have to get out of here," she said.

The look on Davis's face turned to irritation. "You have to get out of here. Just forget you ever saw me."

She started rummaging through Halley's pockets, but he didn't have anything that would open Davis's cell.

"If you really want to help," said Davis, "Look up." There was a pipe in the wall over the glass, and the end of it opened up on the ceiling in Davis's cell. "It's knock-out gas. The only way they ever open my cell is if I'm out. See if you can do something about it."

Fiona nodded and followed the pipe around the corner. It connected to what must have been the machine that pumped the gas in. It had a gas tank inserted in one end. Fiona loosened it and quickly tightened the valve so that she wouldn't knock herself out. She put it back into place and hoped it looked normal.

"It's done," she said.

"Good. Now get out of here."

She wanted to, but there was more thing she had to do. Despite Davis's protests, she started searching the lab for Cheung's vial. She found it on a shelf nestled between all kinds of different chemicals.

Davis's eyes were wild with excitement. "Go, come on!" He pointed at Halley. The man stirred on the ground, and his eyes half-opened.

"Good luck," Fiona said as she raced for the elevator. Halley surged to his feet and charged towards Fiona. She got inside, and the doors closed right before Halley reached her. As the elevator went up, Halley's screams followed her.

Fiona got out of the hospital without anyone seeing her. She was pretty sure that Halley must have been out of the lab by now and that he was following her. It was night, but there was still a fair amount of people about, and Fiona tried to slow down her steps so that she wouldn't look out of place.

Even if Halley's torture had gotten to the most extreme levels, there was no way that Fiona could have given up Cheung. He didn't give her any information on how to contact her. His letter said that he would find her.

But that was a minor concern for the moment. Fiona was in an unfamiliar place without any knowledge of where to hide. She went to the place everyone went when they were in trouble.

Fiona always thought that police stations were more busy at night, but the station here seemed quite serene. In the lobby, a bored receptionist sat behind her desk and read a crumbling, pre-war paperback. Fiona asked if she could see an officer. The woman pointed down the hall without even glancing at Fiona.

She took a seat, and an officer told her that he would be with her in a moment. He chattered on the phone, and it sounded like he was complaining about his ulcers to his doctor. Fiona sat patiently, finally able to relax a little bit and let the strength return to her limbs. The burns on her body where Halley tazed her stung as if she'd been through a scourging.

The wear and tear of the day's excitement started to creep into Fiona's body when she noticed a detective walking towards her. It wasn't the man she talked to at first. He looked more like a hired gun than a cop, and his cold eyes were firmly fixed on Fiona. He snapped his fingers, and another man, just as brutish as his friend, joined him. The first man spoke over a walkie-talkie, and when they got closer, Fiona heard a voice crackle.

"I don't care," the voice buzzed. "Just kill her."

Even with the distortion, Fiona knew it was Halley's voice. Fiona charged down the hallway, and the two goons pulled machine pistols out of their jackets.

The receptionist still sat in her chair reading her book.

"Get out of here!" Fiona yelled, but the receptionist didn't bother listening.

At the first sound of gunfire, instinct slammed Fiona into the floor. The bullets ate through drywall and the receptionist, and the yellowing pages of the paperback fluttered in the air, a single bullet hole stabbed right through their center. The glass doors and windows of the entrance splintered into millions of sparkling points of light. Fiona crawled behind the desk to get cover from the second wave of gunfire.

The receptionist still sat in her chair, and from Fiona's angle, she didn't look dead. The exit was only a few steps away, but every time Fiona tried to run for it, her muscles froze. The gunfire hammered her ear drums, and the dust it threw up choked her lungs. She knew she had only one option, so she waited for a lull in the shooting.

When it came, she hurtled out the door, broken glass crunching under her feet. Another gun shot screamed towards her. It plowed into the concrete walkway, and Fiona tripped as she tried to get out of its way. She ate dirt, giving the goons time to catch up to her. They loomed over her, weapons ready to pump her full of lead.

All three turned to face the street as a car screeched to a halt right in front of them. A woman jumped out of the passenger seat, a submachine gun in her hand. Before the goons could react, she unloaded into them. The unrelenting rain of bullets sent their shredded bodies flying away from Fiona.

"Get in the car!" the woman yelled.

Fiona obeyed, unthinking, and lunged into the back seat.

Cops started pouring out of the station. "Go! Go!" The woman yelled, and the vehicle shot off before she had even gotten all the way inside.

"You're bleeding," she said a few moments later. She tossed a handkerchief at Fiona.

Fiona looked down at her body. In her palms, she found dozens of tiny shards of glass, and her knees looked as if they were dragged across a cheese grater. She didn't feel any pain, however. The dizzying whirl in her head prevented that.

"What the hell just happened?" she asked.

The driver stopped at the traffic light and turned around. "We just rescued you," he said.

Fiona looked up into the face of Dr. Robert Cheung.

# CHAPTER EIGHT

Halley made a heck of a racket as he stormed into the laboratory. Wilcox, seemingly much more subdued, stepped off the elevator behind him.

Davis hoped that Halley's noise meant that Dr. Todd got away. Which meant it was probably time to torture Davis for information about Dr. Todd.

"I have it under control," said Wilcox. He marched past Halley and towards Davis's cell.

"She took out my men," said Halley. "I have to get her. I can get her." His voice held a slight degree of pleading.

Davis tried to ignore his body's anticipation of pain and the panic trying to get to him. "The only girl you'll get is in the glossy pages, Halley."

Halley clenched his teeth and tried not to let the steam fume out of his ears. He stepped right up to Davis's glass partition. "Nobody calls them 'the glossy pages.' Nobody even reads magazines anymore, you idiot."

Davis just smiled and nodded at Halley. There was a time, right after the war, when Davis thought he could disappear, have a new beginning, and forget that he forgot everything about his life. Then one Second Lieutenant Halley knocked on his door, told him that a General Wilcox was interested in offering him a job. The next thing he knew, Davis was in a glass cell that would become his home.

The glass wall stopped Davis from punching Halley in the nose, but at least he could insult him. And it was easy enough; Halley had a fragile ego.

"I think you know the drill," said Wilcox. "What did that girl tell you?"

"Just bring the pain," said Davis. "Zombies ate me alive. Whatever Halley can do is nothing compared to that."

Wilcox smiled and bobbed his head. "Let's try this. Maybe we'll relax some of our stricter rules. Let you go outside once in a while."

Davis didn't really know Dr. Todd, but nothing would get him to talk about her. "I haven't seen the sun in ten years. You think you can tempt me with it? I'm not your dog. I don't do what you tell me. You have Halley for that."

Halley made a move like he was going to tackle Davis, but he rapped his knuckles against the glass. Blood leaked from under broken skin, and Halley backed down.

"She's made life difficult for Major Halley," said Wilcox.

"Good," said Davis. "I always thought Halley's talents were wasted wiping your ass."

The general nodded lazily. He motioned towards the far end of the lab, and two orderlies came running. They carried the usual restraints with them.

"Time to put this dog down?" asked Davis.

As he turned to leave, Wilcox smiled at Davis. "No, you still have some uses."

The general made a quick exit, leaving Halley and the two orderlies. The two stood on either side of Halley and waited for Davis to get into position.

A few moments passed before Halley spoke. "Please, turn around. On your knees."

The growling of the zombies became deeper, throatier. It was the same sound they made when they sensed a threat nearby. "There's no point." said Davis. "You have your knock-out gas."

"I don't want your melon popping open on the floor when you fall," responded Halley with a sneer.

Davis shrugged. He believed Halley. They may have hated each other, but Halley seemed to really enjoy having Davis for the occasional torture session. What would he do if Davis died?

Davis turned around and dropped to his knees. An orderly pressed a button, and the vent in the ceiling started hissing. If Dr. Todd disabled the machine, the gas shouldn't be coming through. He breathed deep to see if he would pass out. He didn't, but he slumped to the floor anyway.

The glass retracted, and the two orderlies entered the cell.

Davis didn't really think anything through. Instinct or rage or maybe boredom forced him to act. He pushed himself into a kneeling position and twisted his torso to stab his elbow into an orderly's knee. The leg locked straight, and a palm strike hyperextended the joint. The orderly lurched forward and smacked his jaw against Davis's bed.

The second orderly bear-hugged Davis and lifted him off the ground. Halley ran into the cell, and Davis kicked at him as he drove his head into the orderly's face. He felt the orderly's teeth cut into his scalp, but he missed Halley.

He continued with the backwards headbutts until the orderly fell against the wall and struggled to breathe through the blood and cracked teeth. Finally, the orderly released Davis and slumped to the ground.

Halley put up his hands, and Davis mirrored his move. They circled each other, neither of them wanting to make the first move. The repeated attack on the orderly took its toll on Davis, and the dizziness made it difficult to see Halley.

Davis needed time to clear his head. "You're not the only killer in this room," he said.

"I'm not a killer," Halley said with tears almost welling up in his eyes. It was not the response Davis expected.

"You are a killer, and so am I." Somehow, it felt good for Davis to say that out loud.

The sorrow in Halley's eyes evaporated in a sudden blaze of anger. Halley stormed at Davis, flailing his arms and screaming as if all sanity had left him. The attack was too much for Davis, and he fell under Halley's wild swings, and Halley followed him to the ground.

The ferocity of the attack could have overwhelmed Davis, the pain could have forced him to surrender, but in his years of captivity, Davis learned patience. Halley was uncoordinated, uncontrolled. He wasted energy trying to break Davis's skull when simpler attacks would have penetrated Davis's defense.

With every strike, sweat and spit flew from Halley's face, and each of his breaths were shorter and sharper than the last. His punches came with the same speed, but they lost their intensity. To compensate, Halley started his punches with his fists high above his head. It was there that Davis found his opportunity.

Davis drove his open palm up and into Halley's jaw, clicking the teeth together with a loud crack. His fingers wormed their way into Halley's eyes, and Halley wailed when fingernails scraped against the whites. He tore himself away from Davis.

Davis jumped to his feet. Tears streamed from Halley's eyes, temporarily blinding him. Davis thrust his foot into Halley's gut, and his foot sank so deep it could have come out the other side. The power in the kick sent Halley flying into the wall behind him. He slumped to the floor.

Davis ended the fight by crushing his knee into Halley's face and ricocheting the head off the wall.

The orderlies moaned in pain, but Davis knew they were out of the fight. They were young guys, too young to remember much from the war. They didn't have the fighter's instincts that Davis and Halley learned back in the day.

Davis exchanged his pants with Halley's, a non-descript pair that looked more professional than the dirty scrubs he had lived in for the past ten years. However, Halley's shoes were too small, and Davis had to take a pair from one of the orderlies. He wiped the blood from his face, head, and hands on his old pants, and completed his outfit with a spare lab coat Dr. Cheung always left lying around.

He went to the elevator and pressed the up button. Any of his fatigue faded under the strange elation he felt pushing that button. The doors opened and he stepped inside, and when the doors closed, they cut out the sound of the growling zombies. Davis smiled. The last bit of the war was finally behind him.

Davis didn't know what waited for him above, and he didn't care. It could have been a thousand bullets headed at him faster than sound, just as long as he was away from the lab. The elevator rose higher, and Davis realized that the air smelled different. The rot of zombies was so normal he forgot there was anything else.

The elevator bounced to a stop, and a bell rung to announce its arrival. One soldier stood in front of the doors, probably expecting to see Halley. At the other end of the hall stood another guard. His back was turned, but that wouldn't last long.

Davis grabbed the soldier's rifle at either end and pulled it straight up and into the soldier's chin. A bit of tongue popped into the air after his teeth were forced shut. He didn't have more than a second or two before the other soldier turned around, and he sprinted down the hall.

The soldier wheeled around and let off a single shot just as Davis collided with him. With an extra shove, he forced the soldier into the wall where he pummeled him with knees and elbows. When the soldier was out of the fight, Davis searched the man's pockets and took his wallet.

A little whimper caught Davis's attention. A nurse stood only a few feet away from him, looking as if she were about to shit herself.

Davis pointed his finger at her. "You go find a corner to hide in until I say you can come out."

The nurse nodded and ran off.

With his head down and hands in his pockets, Davis searched for the exit. It had to be night time, he thought. He only saw a few people walking around, and none paid him any attention. Up until that point, he only assumed night came when the lights in the laboratory faded.

He didn't get too far when the alarm sounded. The nurse. He resisted the urge to start running, but when he saw a group of people, he found his opportunity to escape. He joined them and they lead him straight to the hospital's exit.

There were no police gathering in front of the hospital, but their vehicles patrolled the streets in force. They must have been on the hunt for Dr. Todd.

He wished her luck but didn't bother to think too much about it; he had to escape. But for the moment, he enjoyed the night air filling his lungs and the stars twinkling above. He gazed at the sky, and wondered at its tranquility.

# CHAPTER NINE

Dr. Cheung and his friend took Fiona to an abandoned house about a mile away from the military base. Even though the surrounding houses and the facade of Cheung's house looked decrepit and almost haunted, the inside was fairly clean and devoid of the must of time and weather. If they had any lights, they kept them off, but the glow of the moon through the broken windows was enough. Fiona stood out of the way in the corner of what was once a living room while the woman paced around and talked to Dr. Cheung.

"We can't stop here," the woman said. "They'll eventually start looking for us out here. And we can't trust her."

"We have time," said Cheung. He was the same person Fiona remembered from long ago, the same voice, the same face, but there was something different about him, as if he had taken off a mask. "Nothing has changed."

The woman mocked him with her laugh. "Nothing's changed? Something big is going down, and you know it. We shouldn't be babysitting this girl."

"We can't change that now, can we?"

Fiona stepped forward. "Excuse me. What the hell is going on? And who are you?"

"This is my assistant, Megan Ramecker," said Cheung.

"I'm Dr. Fiona Todd," said Fiona. She felt like she was in an absurd meet-and-greet.

The woman shrugged. "Well, now that we know each other, we should get moving."

Cheung held up his hand. "Not yet. I have to talk to Fiona first. Can you wait for us in the other room?"

Ramecker's eyes glanced between Cheung and Fiona and back. She sighed and left the room.

"Did you get my vial?" asked Cheung.

Fiona nodded and handed it to him.

He snatched it from her hand and quickly read the label, a smile spreading across his face. He opened the top of the vial and drank the contents, smacking his lips when it was done.

Fiona's jaw dropped. "What did you just do?"

"I took what was owed me."

"What do you mean by that?"

Cheung licked the top of the vial. "This is the future. This is the result of the research General Wilcox had me do. It's what will bring humanity through the coming trials. And he denied me what was my right." There was a snarl just barely hidden under his voice.

Without a doubt, this was not the same Dr. Cheung Fiona met after the war. His years in hiding, working for Wilcox, changed him. "What trials?" Fiona asked.

Cheung looked up at her, and for a moment he was his old self again. "There's another war coming."

Fiona's heart shriveled, and her stomach tried to escape through her throat. She looked for a chair to sit on, but the room was empty of furniture. She chose to lean against the wall instead.

"You have done what I've asked of you," said Cheung. "I can get you away from here. You can hide. Maybe you can survive this war."

Fiona already survived a war. To her, survival meant lying, stealing, and killing just to stay ahead. The war forced Fiona to carry scars that only she could see. She needed to do something to erase those scars. "What are the other options?"

The night outside was deadly silent, but Cheung still cast a cautious glimpse outside. "You can stay here. Work with me."

"And what would we do?"

"I can't tell you until I have your answer. If you join me, you'll have to let go of everything in your past."

Maybe letting go of the past was the thing she'd been looking for all along. She nodded.

"It won't be easy."

"Nothing ever is."

One minute later, they were back in the car and driving east. Ramecker had the wheel now, with Cheung in the passenger seat and Fiona in the back. Cheung looked forward at the slowly lightening sky. He spoke to Fiona, or maybe to himself, or maybe to no one. In the sunlight, he looked unusually pale, and a thin layer of sweat glistened on his face.

"When I first met General Wilcox, he was not the man he is now. He was honorable, strong, brave. But the war changed him. I mean, it changed us all, but it changed him differently. He never had a family of his own. He kept his friends at a distance. He didn't really lose anything like the rest of us did. I don't know, maybe he never changed. Maybe the rest of the world changed around him.

"When the Army found me after my injuries, that was the first time I'd seen Wilcox since the start of the war. I'd never seen the man so alive. Everyone else was so beat down they might as well have been zombies themselves. But the war invigorated him. Like he was born for it.

"After I invented my weapon, everyone was so excited, including the general. We were finally able to go on the offensive against the zombies. The war ended, and everyone celebrated. Except Wilcox. During the war he was full of life. In the aftermath, he was nothing.

"I've never asked him, but I have a feeling that the general thinks ending the war was a mistake. My invention was a weapon against the zombies, but it could've been used as a weapon against other people. Make them beg for the weapon, make them prostrate themselves before Wilcox, until he let them have just a little taste of the weapon. Just enough to keep them safe until Wilcox needed something from them.

"But his sadness over the war ending was short lived. He learned something. And he shared his new knowledge with me. And suddenly we saw a way that we could shape the future. For the better, of course." The color returned to his skin as he spoke.

"And what was it?" asked Fiona.

Her voice startled Cheung. He turned around in his seat. "If I told you, you wouldn't believe it. You'd have to see it yourself."

Dr. Cheung didn't seem to want to discuss any further, and Fiona didn't feel like pressuring him. She wondered what she got herself into, how much danger she now faced. Yes, Cheung was different, but that was what time did to people. Fiona was convinced that she made the right decision.

The miles passed, and the sun rose higher in the sky. And those miles were filled with empty houses and burned out buildings. Back when the war started, it was filled with millions of people, all locked in by mountains and bad LA traffic. It must have been a slaughter, thought Fiona. And yet, she caught glimpses of new settlements popping up, green fields providing for the new world. They didn't need another war.

Ramecker continued down the road, through a mountain pass, and into the desert and through a ghost town.

"Palm Springs," mused Cheung. "A long time ago, it was the favorite vacation spot of Hollywood stars. I was planning on buying a home here for my retirement."

"I met a movie star once," said Ramecker. Her voice startled Fiona. She'd been so silent the whole drive, and she spoke with an air of sadness. "It was during the war. In person, he was just a really normal guy. Zombies didn't care that he was famous." She shrugged.

Despite the somber way that Ramecker told her story, Fiona felt a smile starting to form on her mouth. She didn't know what Ramecker or Cheung went through during the war, but she realized that it was probably the same kind of things she went through. Maybe whatever pain she carried within her, the others carried it, too. Maybe she wasn't as alone as she thought.

They continued on into the empty desert wilderness. Fiona wondered if the car could handle the terrain, but eventually they reached a large quonset hut right in the middle of nowhere. There were already a few other cars parked outside. After they parked, Cheung and Ramecker got out of the car. Fiona followed slowly. A generator hummed from the other side of the building.

"Inside this building is something that could change your life," said Cheung. "You may think the idea of it is far-fetched, but believe me when I say that it is real."

"What's in there?" asked Fiona.

Cheung started to speak, then stopped. He thought for a moment then spoke. "When we discovered Davis and his powers, naturally our first thought was that we could find a cure in him. Or at least make a vaccine. So I studied his DNA to look for some kind of anomaly. I found it, and that led Wilcox to realizing that there could be something in this world with more potential to be a weapon than Davis himself."

"What was it?"

Cheung held up a finger to tell her to wait. "Wilcox sent teams all over the world to search, and I did, too. In secret. I found it before him."

Ramecker opened the door into the building. Cheung and Fiona stepped inside. There were about a dozen people inside. Most worked at computers, but a few studied an object in the center of the building.

A soft blue light emanated from a smooth crystal embedded in the top of a metal or stone pillar. The stone twisted and coiled from the ground up to the crystal, like hungry vines or angry snakes. Some kind of inscription or hieroglyphic was carved across the metal in an unrecognizable pattern. A single light raced across each of the symbols, shining across the full spectrum of colors.

Cheung held his hand out to the object. "This is alien technology. Thousands of years, maybe millions of years, more advanced than anything we have."

"Alien technology," Fiona muttered. Ramecker stood behind Fiona as if she expected her to faint. Instead, Fiona approached the object and touched the metal. She didn't even realize she was touching it until she felt resistance when she pushed her hand forward. It was neither hot or cold, smooth or rough. It was like touching air. "What does it do?" she asked.

Cheung chuckled. "Beats me."

# CHAPTER TEN

In the early morning hours, Davis reached his destination. Over the years, Dr. Cheung spoke to him once in a while about a refugee city not far from the base. It sounded like a terrible place to live, but it also sounded like a place where no one would think to look for an escaped science experiment. Cheung's stories provided enough details for Davis to figure out his way to the city.

It was about ten miles away, and it took the whole night to reach it. Davis's endurance surprised him. He did what he could to keep in shape while he was in his cell, but it couldn't have been enough to keep Davis going through the night. Especially after the fighting during the escape.

Davis kept his distance from the city until he knew it was safe to approach. The whole area was enclosed by three massive, concrete walls that butt up against a hill carved out to form a fourth wall. Based on the size, Davis guessed there could be fifty thousand people in there, and if they were packed tight enough, that number could grow to one hundred thousand. The perfect place to hide.

The only entrance or exit in the city was a massive, rusting doorway, the kind that guarded ancient cities in old sword-and-sandal movies. Davis wondered why he could remember those old movies but he couldn't remember his own life. He didn't think too long. Through those large metal slabs was his path to a blank slate.

A line of vehicles and people formed to get into the city. Most were local farmers planning to trade their goods for whatever they could get on the inside. According to Cheung, some of the people would be drug dealers, purchasing from the drug makers on the inside. Apparently, it kept the economy on the inside going and was tolerated on the outside. The rest of the people in line were gamblers, lonely men looking for some action, or other assorted thrill-seekers.

Davis rushed to get into the line, only to wait for the soldiers standing guard to allow admittance as slowly as possible. They checked everyone's IDs and rummaged through all their belongings, finally fitting every entrant with some kind of GPS tracker before they went inside. Davis looked inside his stolen wallet. Two hundred dollars. He hoped it was enough to convince the guard to let him through. And he hoped the nervous shake in his hand didn't make him look too suspicious. His turn to get into the city neared.

A jeep drove along the walls of the city and pulled up alongside the guard's post. Several guards talked for a few moments, then one of them pointed at several of the soldiers idling around. Their sergeant chewed them out for being lazy, and the soldiers jumped to their feet and started surveying the people in the line, studying faces and pacing like hungry tigers.

Were they looking for him? Or were they after Dr. Todd? It was probably both. Davis's face had some good bruises all over it, and he had dried blood all over the back of his head. Whether they recognized him or not, he still looked like a criminal. Silently, he cursed the elation he felt when he stepped out of the hospital and the lack of planning it caused. He turned his body and face ever so slightly to keep himself out of view of the soldiers.

One of them approached, and Davis stepped behind a crate of carrots before the soldier saw him. The owner of the carrots did see him and simply smiled and shook his head. The move was useless. If Davis got to the front of the line, he was caught. If he stayed in line, he was caught. If he made a break for it, they'd probably run him down with their jeep. At least his new cell would provide a change in scenery.

The line stepped forward to within hearing distance of the guards. One of them spoke to a girl, maybe seventeen or eighteen years old, at the exit.

"No one gets out without an ID or GPS," said the guard.

The girl threw up her arms in protest. "I told you, my dad has them. He left without me."

"Maybe he got sick of your face."

"I'm not kidding you. My dad is the cabbage seller who just left like five minutes ago."

"I didn't see any cabbages."

"Because he sold them all. I'm not kidding you."

The soldier put the barrel of his rifle right under the girl's nose. She crossed her eyes to peer down. "I'm not kidding either," said the soldier.

Davis ducked and weaved his way through to the front of the line. He snuck up behind the girl, grabbing her by the shoulders and pulling her away from the rifle. "You'll have to excuse my daughter," he said. "She just wants to see the ocean." Davis pulled the girl through the entrance and into the city.

The girl struggled, but Davis dragged her along until they were out of sight of the entrance and into the refugee city. The streets were dirt, and the buildings were corrugated steel and plywood. Wood fires burned in each of the ramshackle huts, and the smoke almost covered the odor of the trash and filth that seemed to gather in every corner and hole available. The people weren't much cleaner, but they weren't zombies or soldiers. Davis smiled and let go of the girl.

"You ruined my plan," said the girl.

Davis inhaled the pollution, closing his eyes to better concentrate on the unfamiliar smell. "He would have put a bullet through your head," he said, his eyes still closed.

"No. They would have just kicked my ass and thrown me back in here." She poked Davis's arm. "Dude, are you high?"

Davis blinked and shook his head. "What makes you think that?"

"You're obviously not from in here. And for some reason you snuck inside. No one does that."

"How do you know I'm not from in here? There are thousands of people here."

"Anyone on the inside can tell you're from the outside. And I'm pretty sure you're not my father."

"Maybe you should run along and get back to him."

The girl's voice lowered. "It's just me."

Davis regarded the girl. She was a little rough around the edges and dressed like the war was still going on, but otherwise looked utterly normal. He didn't know how trustworthy the girl was, and he didn't know what the refugees thought of outsiders. He wanted to apologize for the bit about her father, but he didn't think she was the type to want an apology.

"Do you guys use this in here?" he asked, pulling cash out of his stolen wallet.

The shine in the girl's eyes gave him an answer before she spoke. "Yeah. We need it to do business with the outsiders."

The money went back into Davis's pocket, and the girl's eyes dimmed. "That's your's this time tomorrow if you help me to disappear in here."

"That's a pretty tall order."

On the outside, Davis's money wasn't much, but he could tell from the girl's face that it was a fortune inside the city. He pulled out some of the cash. "Half up front."

The girl snatched the money faster than a frog's tongue catching a bug. "It's a deal." She checked it to make sure it was real. "So, what crime did you commit outside?"

"I don't remember," said Davis. "And that's the truth. My name's Davis by the way."

"Just Davis?"

"Yeah, one word. Like Madonna." Davis nearly laughed at his own joke.

"Jesus' mom?"

"Yeah. Like that."

The girl stashed her cash in one of the many pouches that adorned her clothes. "I'm Jacey. Where do you want to go?"

There was no discernible plan to the streets in the city. They branched out in crooked lines from the spot where Davis and Jacey stood, and each path looked the same as the last. Davis pointed one way. "Where does that lead?"

Without looking where Davis pointed, Jacey said, "All the merchants from outside gather there. Lot of soldiers standing guard. I don't think you want to go there."

"No, I don't think so. How about that way?" He turned his finger in the opposite direction. The imaginary line that extended from his finger headed down the narrow, rubbish-strewn street and came to rest on a solitary figure dressed in a dirty brown cloak, the hood up to shadow his or her face. Davis didn't have Jacey's sense as to who lived inside the city or not, but he knew that person came from the outside. There was just something about the person, a sense of familiarity.

"Did you hear me?" asked Jacey. She tugged on Davis's sleeve to wake him up. "You really are high, aren't you?"

"What? No." Davis shook his head, but the tangle of lost memories didn't come undone. "What's that way."

"That way leads straight to the center of the city, as long as you don't get lost. It gets pretty rough towards the center."

Without waiting to hear more, Davis headed in. "Let's go."

The figure disappeared, and Davis rushed along hoping to get a second glance. He felt that if he could get a closer look at the person, see its face, some old memory would return.

Jacey raced to catch up. "You're paying me to be your guide. What are you looking for?"

"I thought I saw someone."

"You're an outsider. You don't know anyone in here."

Davis stopped. He felt fine, but Jacey had to gasp for air. "I guess you're right. I don't know anyone on the outside either." He wanted to give Jacey a chance to breathe, but the figure appeared again.

Unconsciously, he ducked behind the corner of a metal hut, yanking Jacey along with him. "There. That person. The one in the cloak."

Jacey took a look. "The guy in the cape? Maybe you did see him from the outside. He's a gangster. They're outsiders, but they pay a lot of money to keep their headquarters in here. They're the only ones allowed to go in and out freely."

"Where's their place?"

Jacey spurt out a laugh. "They're dangerous. Like, they're the leading cause of death in here."

When he was fighting Halley, he said they were both killers, and somehow he knew that it was true, at least for him. And now a gangster, a killer, sparked something in him. A hint at his past? Did his life before the war intersect with killers and criminals?

He had to know. "Take me there," he said.

"You don't know anything about this city, you'll get yourself killed."

"I'll give you the second half of the money. Our deal will be done."

"It's going to take a lot more than money to get me to go to that place."

"I'll owe you a favor."

Jacey shook her head.

"A really big favor." Davis received a blank stare. He pulled out the rest of the money and put it in Jacey's hand. "Keep the money. Just tell me where to go."

"Why's this so important to you?" She pocketed the money.

"I can't tell you."

"Then I can't help you."

For a moment, Davis stared at Jacey. She was really just a kid, and he had no business dragging her along to visit with gangsters. He nodded and left her standing by herself. He picked a street to follow and headed down.

He hadn't gone more than ten yards when a voice called out to him. Jacey ran up to meet his stride. "It's going to have to be a really big favor."

# CHAPTER ELEVEN

The body awoke and remembered that it had already adjusted itself to the planet's environment. The bullet wounds it sustained in the fight with the humans were already healed, and the body felt strong. It sent signals to the mind to wake up.

The mind remained without any activity. There was only a slow trickle of electrical energy between cells, and the bare minimum of chemicals and hormones flowed through to keep the mind alive. The body adjusted its blood flow and sent a rush of nutrients into the mind. Nothing happened.

It tried again, this time including several hormones that would shock the mind into attention. The mind stayed silent. The body tried several more times, each with the same result. The only option was to put the entire being at risk. The body sent all the organs to work producing various stimulants to overload the entire system.

The muscles in the body started to tighten to the point of extreme pain, and they threatened to snap bones and carapace. The chemical imbalances in the body started shutting systems down, and cells started to break apart. The body tried to counteract the damage it had caused by releasing more hormones, but the energy expenditure drove up the body's temperature, further killing more cells.

The mind, deep in hibernation, detected a threat to its existence. It brought itself into awareness and sent signals to the body to shut down any activity. It released chemicals to neutralize those let out by the body. Soon, the body and the mind reached homeostasis.

The Vicious One tried to move, but found itself struggling against pain. Chains, forged from technology developed by its species, held the Vicious One down and glowed with blue electricity. With any movement, the blue would become an angry red and send a burning spasm through the Vicious One's body. The pain was not incredible, but it was enough to discourage further attempts to break the bonds.

Hunger attacked the body. The Vicious One had not eaten since arriving on the planet, and whatever struggle the mind and the body had to wake up drained most remaining energy, and it left the Vicious One in a fog, as if it could not control itself directly. It would need time before it reached full strength again.

The Vicious One was in another human-made structure, a dark, featureless room. The skull of the scholar rested on a pedestal facing the Vicious One, and it was now connected to some kind of engine that pumped nutrients into the skull. The unnatural regeneration of the skull worked overtime to build flesh over the skull, but it was not stable enough to stay on the bone, instead splattering on the ground in a large pile of sludge. A human skittered out of a dark corner of the room and collected the failed skin and fed it back into the engine before hiding away again.

'You have awoken,' said the scholar. The words pierced through the Vicious One's own skull and into its mind.

'You are one of them?' asked the Vicious One. 'One of the Others?'

A rage sharp as fire stabbed through the Vicious One's mind. It only realized after the rage subsided that it felt the scholar's emotions and not its own. 'How do you know that you are not the so-called Others, and we are the pure species?' said the skull. 'Just because you won the war does not mean that you were right.'

The Vicious One wanted to shatter the skull into the floor, but its chains sent wave after wave of searing heat into its skin. Finally, it dropped down. 'You destroyed our homeworlds. All of our culture, our technology, our way of life lost.'

The scholar's amusement echoed through the Vicious One's mind. 'And have you ever seen these homeworlds?' asked the scholar. 'This great civilization you speak of?' It waited for an answer that it already knew, but the Vicious One did not provide it. The skull continued. 'No one has seen any of this. The histories your scholars tell you may as well be myths or dreams. There may have never been any homeworlds. Maybe we are the products of space dust. Formed and evolved in the space between suns.'

'These are all lies meant to weaken our species so that you could destroy us.'

The scholar sent out an emotion that the Vicious One did not recognize. 'Destroy you? We want to reunite our species. Make us whole again. Merge the mind and body into one being, as it should be.

'It is you that have tried to destroy us. When you could have found homeworlds to settle, you instead remained in space to hunt us down. It is no wonder that you now float around on your decrepit ships ready to drift into oblivion within the next generation. You are a decayed civilization.'

The rage the Vicious One felt this time was its own, but it stayed silent and still.

'We offer you a solution,' said the skull. 'Allow the god of gods to enter into you. Become one of us.'

'Your god has no power. If it did, you wouldn't be rotting on this primitive planet.'

'That is only because you have driven us nearly to extinction. But you have never experienced our god. Our god lives in each of us. Its blood flows with ours. It speaks our secret name, and we speak its name. Your gods hide in their celestial clouds never to be seen.'

Something came to the Vicious One's mind. It thought of the skull's life after death, its blood flowing with that of its god. 'The plague. You and the Others are infected.'

'Infected? It is a symbiosis that gives us divinity in the mortal realm. You have bastardized our god into some weapon to use against these humans. Disgusting sacrilege. But all is not lost. Soon, the rest of the species will join with us, and you will see the truth of the universe.'

Somewhere from outside, the Vicious One heard yelling, human yelling. Although unfamiliar with the sounds of human voices, it sounded like the kind of noise associated with violence. There was some kind of struggle outside.

Perhaps the Others had enemies on this planet? The Vicious One had only to wait until an opportunity for escape presented itself. 'Our species can no longer be affected by the plague. How will you carry out your plan?' The Vicious One was beginning to doubt its own convictions. Mere days ago it had asserted that the plague still threatened the species.

The skull did not answer right away, as if it were considering its response. 'You will tell us where your gravity drive is.'

'It arrived here long before we even entered the system. Even before we infected this planet with the plague. Its location is unknown, if it even still exists.' Outside, the sounds of struggle ceased.

'It exists. You would not have been sent here if you did not have a device to summon the rest of the species. Why else would they send scouts here?'

'You know why. We are to determine if the planet is safe for harvesting.'

'Safe?' The Vicious One could feel the skull's mockery in its mind. 'You just said the species is no longer affected by the plague. Are they afraid that it will awaken something within them.?'

The scholar's plans became clear to the Vicious One. 'You intend to summon the invasion force. You will infect them and turn them to your cause. If that is the case, then there must still be infected humans on this planet.'

The scholar's skull projected its joy. 'You can tell us where the gravity drive is. Or not. Even as we speak, I have teams searching the globe for it. Others like me will eventually feel its presence as it disrupts this world's gravity field. The only difference between the options is time.'

The Vicious One's mind almost shut down, but the body forced it to stay alert. The species was doomed. If they invaded the planet, the Others would find some way to transform them into monsters. If they did not invade, they would starve in space. But there was only one choice. More than ever, the Vicious One needed to be free from its chains. It had to destroy the gravity drive. It would be better for the species to die with dignity in space than to become enslaved to a false god.

The woman, the leader of the humans who captured the Vicious One, entered the room. The corruption emanating from her nauseated the Vicious One. She spoke to the skull in her human language. If the scholar responded, it was probably directly into the woman's mind where the Vicious One could not listen.

The woman bowed low, then wrapped herself in a cloak that covered her from head to toe. She made a quick exit. The presence of her corruption was only gone for a moment, but another replaced it, coming towards the room.

Several humans entered. Most of them were armed, but two were captives. The Vicious One believed the first was a female, smaller and younger than the other. The second was male. He was the new source of corruption.

The female stared at the Vicious One. It did not know human expressions, but the female's surprise and horror at seeing an extraterrestrial being was apparent no matter the planet of origin. The male hardly noticed the Vicious One. He strained to look for the corrupted woman that just left, as if they were connected somehow.

The two prisoners were forced to their knees. After a moment, the guards yanked the female to her feet and dragged her out of the room. The male struggled to follow her, but another human rammed its rifle into his gut. He collapsed, spitting out air and bile.

The two remaining guards took up positions on either side of the male. His eyes slowly opened as, the Vicious One assumed, the skull spoke to him. The male remained on the ground, but his eyes became more alert. His muscles became more tense.

He lashed out with his legs, bringing one of his captors to the ground. He retrieved that one's rifle and emptied it into the other before that one even knew anything was happening. He smashed the living guard's head in with the butt of the rifle.

The scholar projected fear and anger and confusion. Its telepathic speech became unfocused, and it spoke to both the male and the Vicious One. The words were in the human language, but the Vicious One recognized the pleading tone.

The human ripped the skull off its pedestal, and the nutrient tubes came loose and sprayed their filth all over the room. The scholar's attendant skittered back out of its corner to attack the male, but he just kicked the attendant to the floor.

With a mighty heave, the human hurled the skull into the wall. Its slimy skin sprayed out in all directions, and a large crack opened up at its base. Holding the rifle like a club, the male attacked the skull until it split in two. The Vicious One could feel the scholar's emotions vanish from its mind.

The human reloaded his rifle and examined the Vicious One for a moment. He raised his rifle. At this range and in its depleted state, the Vicious One knew that it would not be able to recover from the gunshot wounds. It started to speak its secret name when the gun fired.

The bullets hit the chain's power source. The current flowing through them did not die, but they lessened. The human said something and dashed out of the room. His gunfire continued as he fought against more of the Others' human servants.

The Vicious One strained against its bonds. They still sent pain into the body, but the chains were weakening. It would take all of the Vicious One's remaining energy to break free, but there were three humans in the room that would make a good meal.

# CHAPTER TWELVE

Another gangster popped his head around the corner, and Davis popped a bullet into the man's face.

He was in a building full of gangsters trying to kill him, Jacey was off to get executed, there was a monster in chains just a few yards behind him, and a skull just talked to him telepathically. But the only thing that Davis could think about was the woman that passed by on his way in as a captive. She tried to keep in the shadows, and she pulled the hood of the cloak low over her face, but what Davis saw brought back the memories.

That day in the forest, so long ago, with Wolff and the zombies. The day that haunted his dreams every night since. His last memory of his old life and the first of the new. Was that woman really Elise? How could she possibly end up in the same place as Davis, be involved in the same crap as him? She could only be here if everything started at a time before Davis's memory loss.

He had to find her, he had to find out.

Davis charged down the long hallway of the gangsters' hideout, a large building that looked dilapidated on the outside but was quite structurally sound on the inside. It even smelled of fresh paint. Jacey took Davis there as promised, but somehow the gangsters knew that they were coming. And then they took him to that skull.

It promised him things. Power, immortality. The usual things used to tempt others. Davis didn't care or really understand. He figured English wasn't the skull's first language. But then it showed him things. Put the images straight into Davis's brain. Distant planets and strange creatures. Davis felt the zombie blood flowing through his veins, burning away his old self and replacing it with something else. He didn't transform into a zombie, he became something else. A higher being. The ravages of pain ate away at his flesh, but he felt an even greater joy and pleasure as he consumed the lives of others.

The only price to pay was to accept something inside of him. Davis couldn't describe it. It was like a profound emptiness, a complete blindness, yet it had a physical form that suffocated Davis with its awesome might and infinite malevolence.

For a second, Davis knew, without a doubt, that accepting that thing into him was the right answer. He could surrender completely to it, and and all his mortal concerns would be washed away. He would be made anew, greater than he could ever hope to achieve as a normal human.

But then Davis would have just traded Wilcox's prison for another. No matter what, he would have been someone's slave.

Two gangsters barreled towards Davis, blasting spurts of hot lead in his direction and shooting the floor and walls. With splinters of woods stabbing into his skin, Davis ducked into an alcove. He dropped low and rolled out from his cover and shot through the gangsters' feet and knees. They tumbled to the ground where Davis's continued shooting impacted their bodies.

The fight to reach the ground floor was the same, and Davis quickly filled the hideout with dead bodies, blood, and bullet holes. It unnerved Davis at how easily he killed everyone, but then the thoughts of that woman or Elise or whoever she was pushed anything else away.

Davis emptied his rifle into a gangster and tossed his spent weapon aside. Behind him, a door squeaked open. It was the entrance to the stairwell and Davis's path out of the gangsters' hideout. Another enemy started to emerge from the doorway.

There was no time to retrieve a new weapon. Davis slammed himself into the door, crushing the gangster between it and the wall. The man tried to retreat, and Davis let him for just a moment, then he forced the door closed again, trapping the gangster's arm. The bones smashed with a sloppy, wet crunch, like vegetables getting stomped underfoot, and the limb drooped, lifeless.

The gangster plead for his life and another voice said to open fire. Davis dropped out of the way right before the bullets came roaring through the door, carrying bits of wood and flesh with them to decorate the walls. The force of the dozens of tiny impacts blew the door wide open, carrying the poor gangster with it. With his broken arm flopping around, the dead body danced backwards marionette-like, shedding blood and meat across the floor and all over Davis.

When the firing stopped, Davis jumped to his feet, almost slipping in the red mess that covered the ground. There were three gangsters in the stairwell, and Davis shoved the first he saw over the railing. It was a short fall, but the man landed with a satisfying thump.

Davis buried his fist in the second gangster's throat. Cartilage crumpled under the blow, and the gangster kneeled down trying to cough up a lung. Davis finished him off with a knee to the face that almost sent the gangster's skull between his shoulder blades.

The third gangster fumbled trying to retrieve a fresh magazine from his belt and load it into his empty gun. He let out a soft whimper as Davis yanked the magazine away from the man and shoved it into the gangster's eye. A second strike hammered the magazine deeper into the eye socket and into the brain.

Casually, Davis headed down the stairs. The last gangster coddled an ankle, not knowing what to do with the bone that stuck out through the skin. He saw Davis and held up his hands in surrender. Davis simply took the man's rifle and walked away.

The lobby of the hideout was empty except for one person. The woman stood guard over the only exit. Sunlight from outside silhouetted her, and with her cloak discarded, Davis thought that he even recognized the shape of her body. It had to be her.

"Elise?" he asked. Or said. He wasn't sure which.

"You don't know anything, do you?" Elise responded. She tilted her head, as if she were curious about that revelation.

Off to the left, from beyond an open doorway, Davis heard a girl's scream. Jacey.

"Let her go," said Davis. He raised his rifle and leveled the sights between Elise's eyes.

Elise stepped further into the lobby where Davis could better see her face. "I have all the answers to your questions." Her movements were pure grace, her voice music, her eyes seduction. "You only have to come with me." She stood less than a foot away from the rifle's muzzle.

Davis's strength wavered, and the rifle dipped an inch or two. Jacey screamed again.

The explosion of fire and lead from the rifle should have erased Elise's face from existence, but she grabbed the gun and pointed it out of the way. With incredible strength, she tore the gun from Davis's hands and whipped it around into his gut. The attack lifted Davis off his feet, and he fell down thinking that his insides would melt out of his mouth.

Elise's foot came hurtling towards Davis's face. He rolled away from the kick and stumbled to his feet. Elise threw the rifle at him like a spear, and the weapon lodged itself halfway into the wall. With awkward steps, Davis closed in on Elise. He put all his power into his punches, but Elise floated like a ghost and countered every one of Davis's attacks. She hit like a sword, sharp and heavy, every strike sending pain deep into Davis's body.

Something strangled off Jacey's final scream. Another stabbing punch from Elise knocked the wind out of Davis. He knew that he and Jacey were done for. Elise took a chunk of Davis's hair and held his face up for her to see. He wondered if he looked familiar to her.

Elise pulled her fist back, ready to shove it through Davis's brain. And then she paused. It took Davis a moment to hear it over the rush of blood in his head and the ringing in his ears, but something above was ripping apart the building.

Davis's fist crashed into Elise's face. She let go of his hair and staggered backwards. She looked just as surprised at Davis's strength as he was happy that he could hurt her. She ran to the wall and pulled down on what looked like a fire alarm, but the sound it made was more like an air raid siren. She ran outside, and from the surrounding buildings, hundreds of gangsters, probably on edge from all the gunfire, streamed out into the sun. They didn't just have a hideout, they owned a whole chunk of the city.

The crashing noise soon deadened any other sound, and Davis thought the building would fall on him. The gangsters outside waited, each looking up, while Elise disappeared into the crowd. Then the monster broke through the ceiling. Davis raised his arms to protect himself from the debris, and when the dust cleared, the monster stared right at him.

It regarded him for a second then smashed through the wall and outside. It attacked the gangsters, ignoring all the bullets they put into it. It killed them three or four at a time, rending their bodies with its claws or gnashing them with its teeth.

Davis didn't give much time to watching the monster. He headed through the last doorway towards where he heard Jacey's screams. It was a long hallway that descended at a steady grade. The architecture changed as he went further, as if the hallway came from another structure built long before the building on top.

Then the smell of the air changed. Davis almost didn't notice it because it was the stench he knew every day in his cell. Rotten yet living flesh. Zombies.

The hallway led to a single metal door. It was already open, and Davis burst in, ready for a fight despite the beating Elise gave him. The place was huge, at least one hundred yards across, and dark except for the weak light thrown out by a dozen or so naked lightbulbs. Three men stood at the edge of a pit that made up most of the chamber. Two were the gangsters that took Jacey away, and the third had to be the one who guarded the pit. From the odor and the nauseating growls, Davis knew what was in the pit. And from the way the three men looked down into the pit and laughed and pointed, he knew that Jacey was down there.

As the gangsters exchanged money between their hands, Davis snuck up behind them. He shoved two of them into pit and grabbed the third and brought him to the ground. The two below screamed as the zombies chewed through their bodies, and the third could only cower as Davis gave him a beating that would make getting eaten alive seem merciful.

Hands sore and dripping with gore, Davis stood up and stared down into the pit. There must have been two or three hundred zombies below. And in one corner, Jacey desperately swung an aluminum baseball bat at the undead. It was a cruel game the gangsters were playing, but it kept Jacey alive.

"Hey!" Davis screamed. "Leave her alone!" His voice echoed through the chamber.

The zombies all froze, and those with enough muscle control turned to look up at Davis. The only sounds were the zombies' ragged breaths and the metal plunk of the baseball bat. They hesitated for a moment, like a dog just learning new commands, then turned their attention back to Jacey.

Davis cursed and leapt into the pit. As he expected, the zombies ignored him, as if he were one of them. He kept yelling at them to stop, and each time they stopped for a little longer. But when he reached Jacey, there were still some that ignored his orders.

Tears and snot poured down Jacey's face. She couldn't have been more than a toddler back in the war and didn't have any experience fighting zombies. But still, there were seven or eight zombies laying on the ground with their brains oozing out.

Davis took the bat away from Jacey and used it to send a zombie's head flying out of the pit. "I said stop it."

This time, all the zombies stopped.

"Turn around and shut up," said Davis. The zombies obeyed.

Jacey grabbed Davis's arm. "How the hell is this happening?"

Davis shook his head. "Long story. We got to find a way out of here."

And the way out presented itself. On the opposite end of the pit, two gigantic doors, like hangar doors, slid open, letting in the daylight. The ground sloped back up towards the surface, and Elise stood at the top.

From beyond her, Davis could hear gunfire and the screams of men getting torn to shreds by a monster.

Elise glared down at the zombies, like an evil queen sneering at her subjects. The zombies all stared back. She simply pointed outside towards the sound of the fighting, and her soldiers all marched to her command. The queen found Davis in the crowd and smiled at him.

# CHAPTER THIRTEEN

Looking into the mirror, Halley prodded the tender, swollen parts of his face. It hurt, but it didn't hurt as much as the throbbing headache he had when he finally woke up in the lab. And that didn't hurt nearly as much as the embarrassment he felt when Wilcox found him with a bloody face and no pants.

But none of it hurt as much as the disappointment of letting both Davis and the woman escape so easily. Whatever the woman did to or took from the lab would give Cheung an advantage over Wilcox, and with Davis gone, Wilcox lost him as a source of research. And it's all thanks to me, thought Halley. I let the general down.

His fist smashed into the mirror, and the fractures in the glass spread out like spider legs to the edges. A nice gash opened up on his knuckles, and blood flowed over his fingers to drip into the sink. Halley played with the broken skin for a moment, letting the searing pain drown out any of his thoughts and focus his mind.

If Wilcox didn't want to drive Halley out to the desert and put a bullet through his head, then Halley knew that he had a lot to make up for. Up until now he, as Davis suggested, had just wiped Wilcox's ass. Now, he had to prove that he was a valuable part of Wilcox's plans. Halley knew that he had to start making decisions of his own instead of being Wilcox's butler.

An aide entered the restroom and cautiously approached Halley. "Sir, General Wilcox would like to see you."

Halley nodded to dismiss the aide. He quickly bandaged himself and put on a fresh uniform. Wilcox probably made a decision as to which caliber round would make a better exit wound on Halley's skull. Would protesting his execution prove to Wilcox that he wasn't just a simple lackey?

He found the general alone in the conference room. Wilcox was not mad, he was not annoyed, he was not even a little bit irked. Instead, he smiled at nothing in particular, and his happiness almost glowed off of him.

Halley stood at attention. "Sir, the escape of both the woman and Davis are entirely on me. If you need me to . . . resign my post, I will take care of it myself." He paused and waited for an answer, but Wilcox didn't speak. "Of course, if you wanted to resign me yourself, that is acceptable. Sir."

"No. It doesn't matter," said Wilcox. "Everything is going according to plan." He slid a tablet computer across the table towards Halley. The screen displayed a map with a little blinking dot on it. "It's a GPS tracker. When I'm satisfied that it's reached Cheung's hideout, then I've got him. I was always planning on letting the woman go after you finished with her. But the escape makes it more believable."

Halley didn't exactly feel relieved, but at least there was no execution in the foreseeable future. "What about Davis?"

Wilcox gave Halley his serial killer grin. "I have enough from him that I'll be able to get him myself later." The general's grin grew wider, and he started to squeeze his hands into tight fists. The effort was so great that Wilcox's veins started to distend on his neck.

Halley wanted to know more, but Wilcox's secretary stepped into the conference room. The general relaxed his hands.

"Sir, this is an emergency," she said. "There are reports of a battle in the refugee city."

Wilcox snorted. "There's always a battle in that slum."

"The guards are reporting that a giant creature is killing all the people inside."

Both Wilcox and Halley straightened up. "Have they closed off the city?" asked Halley.

"Yes, sir."

"Good. Get out of here," said Wilcox. After the secretary left, he turned to Halley. "You need to kill that alien. When that is done, you need to shut down that city. No one that saw that alien is allowed to leave. Make sure any of our men that saw it can guarantee their mouth will stay shut. You know what to do if they can't."

Halley nodded, slowly, as if he were bowing down in front of a god. So there would be more killing. But if it protected more people than it hurt, it would be justified. Right? "What about civilian casualties?" he asked.

"They're refugees, not civilians."

With that, Halley left and assembled his fleet of helicopters. A few of the vehicles were military, but most of them were civilian models repurposed for fighting. As long as there was a way to strap a gun on the bird, it was useful.

Halley's own chopper was an old private helicopter converted for his own uses. He had machine guns mounted on either side of the cabin and most of the interior space modified to hold the various bombs Halley carried in his chopper. His crew consisted of a pilot and a gunner.

Within ten minutes of receiving word of the alien in the refugee city, Halley took off, accompanied by seven other helicopters. By air, it was not that long to the refugee city, and Halley was just in time to see something he thought he'd never see again. He leaned out the side of his helicopter to get a better look.

One building had a giant opening on its side that led into a dark pit. From out of it, zombies shambled into the light. They moved slowly at first, but upon seeing all the fresh people around them, they used what little strength their ruined muscles had to pounce on anybody they could.

The memories of the war storming back into his mind distracted Halley for a moment. It took time for him to even notice the giant alien surrounded by dozens of dead bodies and standing in a slop of mud and blood and guts.

So, Wilcox was telling the truth about aliens. Halley was surprised that he didn't have much reaction to the alien. It should have been a moment that changed his whole perception of his place in the universe, but he didn't really care. He only cared about the zombies. Killing them would be the first step towards getting back onto Wilcox's good side.

A voice buzzed over the radio. "Sir, are those zombies?"

Halley nodded even though the other man couldn't see him. He had to make a decision. "All right. Open fire. Everyone, open fire. If it moves, kill it. Doesn't matter if it's a man, woman, child, or animal. Destroy it." As far as he was concerned, everyone down there was already lost. Making the order was simple. It was what Wilcox would have wanted.

The pilot brought the helicopter to a hover. The gunner on Halley's helicopter pointed his giant machine gun down into the crowd of zombies and pulled the trigger.

Underneath the rain of hot metal, a red mist filled the air and slimy zombie chunks scattered up and down and left and right. Humans and zombies all fell, but it was not enough. Some of the zombies broke through and ran into the city streets. And in the confusion caused by all the gunfire, the alien disappeared.

"The zombies are getting away," Halley told his pilot. "Bring us over some of those buildings."

The pilot directed the vehicle over. Halley and his gunner grabbed a crate of explosives. It was filled with Molotov cocktails. The scarcity of any sophisticated explosive device forced the military into using improvised devices. Halley just felt primitive using the weapon, but the thought of zombies burning brought a warm feeling in him.

He and his gunner lit up the bombs and started tossing them outside the helicopter. The cocktails shattered on rooftops and fire spread out from the impact like an orange liquid. They weren't that damaging, but the buildings in the refugee city had a lot of old, dry wood in them. It wouldn't take long.

The pilot maneuvered the helicopter to a new area. Halley pulled out a special weapon of his own design. It was a large glass jug holding five gallons of homemade napalm. Taped to the side of the jug were several bombs that Halley made himself. He looked out the side of the helicopter to judge the distance to the ground and cut the length of the wicks on the bombs.

He lit up the wicks and tossed out his bomb. He never tested the device before, and he hoped it would work properly.

It did. Right above the rooftops the bombs went off. They shattered the glass jug, spraying napalm everywhere and igniting the chemical. Flames spread from the center of the explosion like a halo of death. Far below, the screams of fear from seeing zombies changed into screams of pain as the scorching chemical ate into flesh. Halley grinned.

"Get the second one," he told his gunner.

The pilot flew the helicopter through the thick black smoke that engulfed the city and choked the air, trying to find a clean spot to set ablaze. The gunner lit up the wick and prepared to toss the bomb.

"Holy shit, sir!" the pilot yelled.

Halley glanced outside. The alien stood on a rooftop, glaring at the helicopter, and a large piece of corrugated steel soared through the air like a giant Frisbee. The pilot lurched the helicopter out of the way.

Halley grabbed a hold of anything to keep himself from tumbling out of the helicopter, and so did the gunner. The wick still burned on the bomb and came dangerously close to setting off the device. Halley rammed his foot into the gunner's stomach and sent him and the bomb out of the helicopter.

The gunner only fell a few feet before the bomb exploded. A wave of scalding napalm flowed into the helicopter. Halley got lucky and managed to avoid getting covered in the stuff. The pilot, however, shrieked as the napalm bathed his head in its magma-like heat. His face slagged off his skull and splashed over the helicopter's instruments.

As the liquid in his eyes vaporized, the pilot wrenched deliriously at the controls. The helicopter careened down towards the refugee city, and Halley had to use every ounce of his strength to avoid the little meteors of napalm jelly that sloshed around the inside of the helicopter.

As the helicopter plummeted, the pilot let out a final screech before the napalm slithered down his throat. Halley tried to pray, but he forgot how.

# Chapter Fourteen

To Davis's surprise, Elise didn't order any of the zombies to kill him and Jacey. She emptied them all out into the refugee city and even left the door open.

"Are you okay?" Davis made a quick check of Jacey, looking for any bite marks. He doubted that she could survive it the way he did, and if she was bitten, it would be easier for him to turn the baseball bat on her now rather than later. But she only had a few scratches from getting thrown into the pit.

"How did you do that?" she asked again. Her eyes stared blankly at Davis. "How did that woman do that?"

"Her name is Elise. Elise Weiss, I think." The name just popped into his head. "She does it the same way I do, I suppose."

"What do you mean?"

Davis rolled up his sleeve, revealing the scars. Jacey traced the bite marks with her fingers. She may not have had any clear memories of the war, but she knew what the scars meant.

"That's impossible. You should be . . ."

"Dead?"

"One of them."

Davis covered up his arm. Then, as if by instinct, he fell to the floor and the thunderous rumble of machine gun fire blasted in his ears. He and Jacey curled up as small as possible, becoming smaller targets, but Davis soon realized that the gunfire came from outside.

A dozen gangsters ran into the pit to find cover, each of them bleeding or missing limbs. A dozen zombies followed them in.

Davis took care of the zombies first. It was easy enough. They were too distracted by the gangster dinner buffet. Taking care of the gangsters was easy, too. He didn't know if their injuries came from the zombies or from the gunfire, but they were his enemies.

The last gangster's head opened up underneath the baseball bat. "We got to find a way out of here, Jacey."

The girl stared at him as if he were a zombie intent on eating her. She held her hands over her mouth, but whether it was to stifle a scream or hold in her puke, Davis didn't know.

"It's not safe here," Davis said. "Not in this city." He held out a hand but Jacey backed away. "I'm sorry you had to see that. But this is war."

Davis waited a second then headed for the exit. He heard Jacey's footsteps following behind him. The gunfire was done, and now several helicopters hovered over the city dropping fire bombs. It has to be Wilcox, Davis thought. The fires flowed over the flimsy buildings, sending up thick clouds of black smoke. The agonized pleas for death from the burning refugees were almost as loud as the gunfire from moments ago.

The grime of ruined bodies covered every square inch of the ground. Every step squeezed blood out of the dirt, and Davis felt like the ground would suck in his foot, then his body, and drown him in gore. Some of the people and zombies still moaned, but their bodies were so destroyed that they were as good as dead.

Smoke clouded Davis's vision, but occasionally a helicopter would fly overhead, and its rotor blades would clear away the smoke. He saw some people walking around, each of them stumbling through the battlefield and their own dazed minds. Davis wondered if Elise was still walking or if she lay in shreds on the ground. He had a feeling that she got away just fine.

From out of the haze, a gangster approached Davis and Jacey. The cloak marked him as a gangster, but there was something wrong about the way he walked. Davis moved closer to him.

"Just leave him alone," said Jacey.

Davis stopped the gangster in his tracks by poking him in the chest with the bat. The man had the clouded, dead eyes of a zombie. But that was impossible. It took hours, sometimes days, for the transformation to finish. The gangster couldn't have been bitten more than a few minutes ago.

"I think we really need to get out of here," said Davis. "And fast." He pulverized the zombie and looked around for a good exit.

"I have no idea where we are," said Jacey.

A helicopter flying overhead pushed away all the smoke. Davis and Jacey followed its path. It zig-zagged through the air, and fire filled its cockpit. Just as the smoke started to fill Davis's eyes again, the helicopter plummeted towards one of the city's outer walls. The ground shook as the helicopter made its final landing.

"Do you think it broke through the wall?" Davis asked Jacey. Without waiting for an answer, he said, "Can you take us to the crash?"

Jacey nodded and led the way. She found a path that was mostly untouched by the fire, but they didn't encounter any other people. Inside the buildings, however, Davis heard the crunch of bones and the squishy ripping of flesh as zombies nourished themselves. And in some buildings, dead bodies convulsed and rattled as the fever set in and the final transformation began. If the zombie gangster was any indication, it was only a matter of moments before a new generation of zombies walked the earth.

They found the helicopter shortly, and its crash took out a chunk of a nearby building, But more importantly, it left a giant crack in the city wall. Davis worked his way around the burning remains of the helicopter to inspect the crack. In one spot, he could see straight through to the outside.

"Maybe we can dig through," Davis said, hitting the wall with the bat. "Find something we can use as a pick axe or whatever."

Jacey went searching, but never strayed outside of Davis's sight.

"Help," a weak voice said. Davis had to stop smashing the bat into the wall to make sure he heard the voice. It came again.

Davis found the source of the voice and almost burst out laughing at what he saw. Even through the swollen face, he recognized Halley. He looked whole, except for his left arm pinned under a huge chunk of cement. The flesh was broken through to the bone, but the bone looked intact.

Halley came to his senses and focused his eyes on Davis. "Dammit."

The temptation to kill the man was great, but the desire to escape was greater. "Do you have anything I can use to blow up this wall?" Davis asked.

"You have to help get me out of here." Halley made an order more than he made a request.

He wasn't sure if he should help. Dropping the bat on Halley's face would have been more fun. "Fine," Davis said. He shoved his fingers under the piece of cement and tried to lift, but the piece was too heavy. He tried again and gave up. "Do you have a knife?"

Halley sat up so fast he could have ripped his own arm off. "Are you crazy? I'll bleed out."

Jacey walked up behind Davis. "Oh my God, who is this?"

"An old friend," Davis and Halley said together. Davis faced Jacey. In one hand she held a long piece of steel, and in the other she held a giant glass jug that looked like a bomb. The goo that leaked out of a small crack smelled like gasoline.

"Is that napalm? Is this what you were going to use to blow the wall?" asked Davis. Halley didn't answer.

Davis grabbed the jug from Jacey and walked away.

"You can't just leave him," Jacey said, following him.

"I just did." He looked for the best spot to place the explosives.

"Please."

Davis looked at Jacey. Earlier in the day he said that he would owe her a big favor. After everything that happened to her and her city, he knew that there was nothing he could do to repay her. With a sigh, he picked the jug back up and headed towards Halley.

"Whoa, whoa. What are you doing?" asked Halley.

Davis, careful not to get any napalm on himself, smeared a huge dollop of the stuff on Halley's arm, right where the bone showed through. He found a piece of wood with a bit of ember on the end and blew on it to make it glow orange. "This is really going to hurt."

Halley screamed at such a high pitch Davis thought it was Jacey. Then he realized Jacey was screaming, too. Davis let the napalm do its work, then he gave a pull on Halley's good arm. The charred bone broke away like old bark off a tree, and Halley came loose.

He flopped around, swinging his flaming stump around and dripping napalm everywhere. Davis tackled him to the ground and started smothering the flames with dirt.

"You bastard," Halley said and fainted.

Davis dragged Halley's limp body to where it would be safe from the blast he was about to set up on the wall.

Searching through Halley's pockets, he found a lighter. He traded the baseball bat for Jacey's steel rod and told her to keep an eye on Halley.

He went back to the wall and used the steel to chip away a little alcove to place the explosives. He had nearly finished his work when the aluminum bat rang against something solid.

Jacey smashed the zombie a second time in the face, ending its unnatural life. From out of the swirling smoke, more of the undead appeared. Some were the old, putrid zombies from Elise's pit, put others were fresh, refugees or gangsters. The newly turned moved with more confidence than their rotten kin, their muscles strong and healthy, their guts ready to find their first meal.

Davis gave the lighter to Jacey. "Take care of the wall. I'll hold them off. Just use the explosives. No napalm."

Davis approached the nearest zombie. "Stop right there."

It listened and gazed at him with its blank eyes. In life it would have been a woman, maybe a little older than Jacey. A refugee, but she had her life in front of her. And now the war, reborn, took it all away from her. It never did end, did it? Davis asked himself.

He stabbed the steel rod between her eyes and shoved hard enough for it to come out the other side.

The eyes stayed just as dead, but once the body stopped twitching Davis knew the thing was dead forever.

He ordered the next two zombies to stop, and they obeyed. Then their muscles tensed and started shaking. Their heads started rattling, as if they were trying to shake a wasp out of their skulls. Their eyes rolled, and they started clawing at their own faces, stripping the skin off in long, bloody strands.

Then they returned to normal, stalking towards Davis with even more hunger in their growls. These zombies didn't just find him, Jacey, and Halley, he thought. Elise sent them.

And her control over the zombies was greater.

Davis whipped the steel rod around like a giant sword and brought it down on the zombies' necks, severing their spines with a crack as loud as a tree branch snapping. He ordered the other zombies to go away, but they shook off his commands as fast as he could say them.

With bodies that were alive just minutes ago, the zombies converged on Davis. He lashed out, taking some down, but their numbers were too great, and Davis could only give himself some breathing room.

"Jacey! We have to blow the wall now!"

He speared a zombie through the mouth, its teeth shattering and spilling blood like a busted dam.

"Jacey!"

He spared a moment and glanced her way. She held her zombies off well enough, but the new zombies were quicker and harder to kill than moldering pieces of flesh.

Davis rushed to join her, but his steel rod resisted his movement. The zombie still held it in its mouth, and now it was trying to wrench the weapon out of Davis's hand. Davis fought back, ripping the rod forcefully through the zombie's cheek. The momentum of the weapon pulled it into another zombie that grabbed it and pulled.

The struggle was enough time for a zombie to get behind Davis and sink its teeth into his shoulder. He let go of the rod and punched his attacker until it released its bite. The wound wasn't deep, but hot blood poured out, infecting the surrounding zombies' senses and sending their instincts wild.

They piled in, nails peeling away little bits of skin, teeth clicking and trying to get a little nip. One latched onto Davis's arm, and he shoved his finger into its face to pop its eye like a water balloon. But as soon as he could get one off of him, another would take its place. Eventually, they tore him to the ground.

Jacey kept fighting, but it would be a matter of moments before the zombies overwhelmed her. As the pain of zombies taking apart his old scars to make new ones started to cloud Davis's mind, he wondered if he would survive and, if he did, would he remember anything? It didn't matter, the war was ending at last.

A rock flew through the air and split open a zombie's scalp, giving Jacey a chance to pulp its head. Halley charged into battle, joining Jacey, his one arm holding a sharp chunk of cement. He drove the shard into a zombie's abdomen, tearing open a jagged hole for the viscera to escape. The zombie tripped over its own intestines, bringing another down with it.

Jacey finished those two off while Halley hacked away with his clumsy weapon. Soon, they had just enough time to set the explosives. Halley adjusted the fuse, and Jacey touched the lighter to it.

Together, they jumped behind cover, seconds before the wall exploded. Davis pulled his bloodied arm over his head to protect himself, but he still felt the sting as shards of the wall entered his skin. The force of the explosion knocked most of the zombies off of him, and he kicked away any that remained.

The hole in the wall was just big enough for a person to crawl through. Halley checked that it was safe and crawled through. He held his hand out for Jacey, but she stopped to look for Davis.

"Get out of here," he said. The pain of his wounds prevented him from yelling.

She hesitated, and both Davis and Halley urged her to get out of the city. She still wouldn't move.

"Behind you!" warned Halley. A zombie grasped Jacey and slammed her against the wall. Halley tried to crawl back through the hole, but his one arm couldn't do the job.

Davis surged to his feet. The strain on his muscles opened his wounds further, but he ignored the cold blade of pain. He wrestled the zombie away from Jacey and forced its skull into the wall. He drove it in again and again until its brains oozed out of its nostrils.

"Get out of here," he told Jacey. This time she listened.

The surrounding zombies recovered from the explosive blast and started towards the wall. Davis looked between them and Jacey and Halley, both framed by the hole in the wall. He ran his hand through one of his bite wounds and flicked his blood into the zombies' faces. The he spattered some into the ground around him.

Davis moved away from the hole, and the zombies followed him.

Jacey stuck herself halfway through the hole, but Halley's arm pulled her back out.

Davis ran back into the city, engulfed in smoke and hunted by the undead.

# CHAPTER FIFTEEN

Every time the Vicious One tried to escape over the walls of the humans' prison, their sky vehicles would open fire on it and force it back into the inferno. It had already taken down one of the vehicles, but enough remained to present a danger.

The body could only create so much protection against the fire, but it was safer than facing the weapons of the flying vehicles. Their bullets were enough to damage the Vicious One more than it could heal. And at least the infected humans would all die in the fire.

The Vicious One plunged into the conflagration to hide from humans. The best it could hope for was to wait for the fire to consume all its fuel. Then it could attempt to make a run for it when the opportunity presented itself. Or maybe the rest of the team would see the pillar of smoke and come to investigate.

Its skin dripped with a thick mucus secreted by the body. Flames licked at the mucus, but only a small amount of heat broke through for the Vicious One to feel. The body used too much energy to make the mucus, forcing the Vicious One to find nutrition where it could. There were plenty of dead humans lying about, their skin turned to charcoal and their bones broken from the intense muscle spasms caused by the heat. The flavor did not appeal to the Vicious One. It preferred raw food.

But it was free and easy. It was consuming its eighth or so human when it sensed something. It was difficult to tell at first. The mind had slowed its activities to give more strength to the body, but the feeling was unmistakable. The smell of corruption.

The Vicious One followed the smell until it found the source. As it suspected, it was the woman. Still alive amidst all the death.

Eighty or more infected humans surrounded her, each answering to her orders. The fresh meat on their bodies and the still bleeding wounds indicated that they were recently turned humans, not the decomposing corpses that the sky vehicles initially opened fire on.

The woman sent several of the infected ahead of her to clear burning debris and make a path safe for her to walk. The infected obeyed even though it caused their deaths. The massive weights they moved shredded tendons from muscles or bent joints at the wrong angles. The blistering heat melted the skin from their bones, and yet they kept working until movement became impossible. Then another would take its place.

The Vicious One did not think that humans were advanced enough to protect their own bodies from fire, but the woman seemed unperturbed, and even casual. Perhaps, thought the Vicious One, she has an escape nearby. And if she had an escape, that meant the Vicious One had an escape, too.

The Vicious One followed the woman and her slowly diminishing entourage until they reached the rocky cliff face that formed one of the prison's walls. The Vicious One stayed back and hidden from the woman.

Where once a large building stood, only a pile of orange-glowing rubble remained. The woman sent in the last of her infected slaves to clear the mess. Soon, at the cost of their wretched lives, they unearthed the opening to a large tunnel.

That was the escape route. The Vicious One did not need the woman to lead it through, and her corrupted life was an insult to nature. It stormed from its hiding place, using all its speed to wipe the woman from existence. But it was not enough.

The woman did not even turn to look at the Vicious One. She simply dashed to one side, avoiding the Vicious One's attack and sending it tumbling with its momentum.

The Vicious One quickly recovered and whirled around. The woman stood away from it, not taking any defensive position and seemingly calm. Now that the Vicious One knew the capabilities of the woman, it knew to be more cautious in its attack. She was fast, but no match for its strength.

Something scratched at the Vicious One's leg. It looked down to find a half-scorched infected trying to rip apart its skin. It grabbed the corpse by the head and dashed it into the ground. Then the others started to rise, the woman's desire to defeat the Vicious One so great that it compelled their ruined bodies to move.

The fire should have sent them all to their final death, but their lives persisted. They stood and shambled towards the Vicious One, damaged pieces falling from their bodies. They formed a protective barrier in front of their mistress, and slowly, all the combatants circled until the woman had a clear path to the tunnel.

The Vicious One wanted to attack, but it hesitated. All the scholars and alchemists claimed that the plague would no longer have any effect on the species. But what did they really know? None of them ever left their cloisters. If one of the infected passed its disease on to the Vicious One, what would happen. Would it become one of the Others, a slave of darkness? Would it only be a body with no mind, like the humans?

It did not matter. The rest of the species, the ones still waiting in space, could not be allowed on the planet. The plague threatened their bodies, but the Others threatened their souls.

As the woman disappeared into the darkness of the tunnel, the infected and the Vicious One attacked at the same time. In one swipe, the Vicious One took the heads of three of its enemies. The rest tried to pile on the Vicious One, but it batted them back and into the ground. It stomped on one, popping its skull like a ripe fruit. An infected tried to climb the Vicious One's leg, slipping on the mucus. The Vicious One grabbed it and pulled its torso in half. The organs slopped onto the ground, but a long, thin organ kept the upper and lower halves of the infected connected.

Holding the two halves of the body together, the Vicious One whipped the body around. The long organ trailed behind, dragging the rest of the viscera with it. The organs caught a group of infected and spun around them, tangling them like a fleshy rope.

With a tug, the Vicious One separated the organs from the body halves, and crushed one infected to a pulp underneath the top half. It grabbed each leg by the foot and snapped the piece in half so that it held two improvised clubs.

It laid waste to the infected, ruining their bodies until only a red paste remained. The Vicious One tossed away its weapons and headed into the tunnel.

In the confined space, the woman's corruption intensified and left a trail. But it was not the only corruption. There was something much stronger, more purer, than the woman. Like the skull of the scholar. There were more of the Others deep in the tunnel.

The tunnel became darker, and the Vicious One thought that it would be engulfed in blackness, but it saw a distant light. It quickened its pace and headed there.

In front of the exit were several long vehicles, some kind of motor vehicle with a large rectangular metal box trailing behind it. The Vicious One could smell hundreds of infected bodies inside of each one. Several of the woman's human servants loaded large containers into a smaller vehicle while the woman watched.

The corruption came from those boxes. Skulls of the Others. The Vicious One's mind could not conceive of a way for it to escape the tunnel alive. It had to kill the Others, the woman, and all the infected. The rest of the team would learn of the events here and know of the dangers of the Others.

A wave of energy passed through the air at a frequency familiar to the Vicious One. A vehicle emerged from around a corner. It carried as cargo technology designed by the species but constructed by human hands. It was old technology from generations before the Vicious One was born.

The Vicious One knew missiles when it saw them. It even knew the purpose of the missiles. They carried the plague within. When detonated, they would release the plague into the air and infect whoever it was designed to target.

That was their plan, the Vicious One thought. If they could find the gravity drive, they would summon the rest of the species to this planet They would explode the missiles, corrupting the species. Then the Others would have a new, loyal army, the resources of a harvested planet, and a fleet to spread their corruption across the galaxy.

Something hummed in the Vicious One's mind as one of the skulls reached for it telepathically. The woman opened one of the containers so that she could communicate with the skull. She looked up into the Vicious One's eyes.

The woman shouted at her servants, and they jumped into their vehicles and started them. The rumble of engines echoed up and down the tunnel as the Vicious One headed towards the woman and the Others.

Six of the woman's servants stepped in front of the Vicious One and threw off their cloaks. The corruption of the Others was so great that the Vicious One did not sense it in these six. Their's was just like the woman's, but older and more seeped into their being.

And it showed on their skin. Previously hidden by their cloaks, the deformity of their features now showed. Thick red veins pulsed across their faces, blood flowing underneath like an animal scurrying in its burrow. Their human teeth had fallen out to be replaced with bony growths that resembled fangs. The nails were thickened and hardened, coming to a point as sharp as the edge of a star. And their eyes were dead. Dull and foggy and empty like those of the infected.

The corrupted moved with the same speed as the woman. They were not corpses like the rest of the infected. The Vicious One attacked, but the corrupted scattered and avoided its blow. They moved in, screeching until blood squirted out of their throats, and slashed at the Vicious One with their claws.

They broke through the skin easily and dashed out of the way before the Vicious One could counter. Soon, ribbons of flesh hung from the Vicious One's legs. The body diverted nutrients to the spot, but the healing was slow.

The corrupted were too fast, and with its injuries, the Vicious One knew that it could not hope to chase them down and kill them one at a time. It had to draw them in.

It dropped to the floor and closed its eyes. The moment of rest felt good, and the body took advantage to heal its wounds more efficiently. The corrupted encircled the Vicious One, then all together they closed in.

Heaving against the ground with the might of its limbs, the Vicious One rolled onto its back and smothered two of the corrupted under its carapace. The corrupted squealed and futilely slashed at the hard shell until they had been completely flattened. Their bodies had become a red mush, but the few recognizable parts still twitched as if they were trying to attack the Vicious One.

The remaining four faced off against the Vicious One. They came in at once, and the Vicious One grabbed two and brought their heads together. The skulls merged into one in an explosion of crimson that splattered onto the ceiling of the tunnel and came back down like rain.

But defeating those enemies cost the Vicious One. A stab of pain, hot as the fire back in the prison, gripped its arm. One of the corrupted sank its deformed teeth into the Vicious One's arm. The body could sense a poison with an acidic sting flowing through the fangs and into the body's system.

The pain came again, this time in the opposite leg. With its free arm, the Vicious One swatted the corrupted at its leg away. It lifted the other arm in the air, the corrupted's teeth still holding on, and brought it back down. The corrupted's lower leg bones stabbed through the thighs, but it still held on. Its legs flopped around as the Vicious One again brought it into the air and slammed it down. This time, the corrupted's rib cage smashed into the earth, and the shards of bone pulped the organs inside.

The last corrupted raced towards the Vicious One. The Vicious One swung its infected arm in an upwards arc, catching the corrupted in the groin. Its claws cleaved the corrupted straight through its head, and the opposite halves fell to the ground where the hot guts sloshed out.

The woman and her vehicles were gone. The Vicious One ran out into the sun. Smoke from the fire choked the air and turned the sunlight a deep red. The ground was paved. Some kind of road.

It heard scrambling from behind and turned around. The rest of its team emerged, led by the Pious One.

'You are hurt,' said the Pious One.

The Vicious One examined its arm and leg. Something had already started to soak into its veins like a black mold. 'I am infected.'

It could smell the terror coming off of its companions.

'We all saw the fire,' said the Pious One. 'Then we sensed some kind of corruption and came here. Was that you?'

'No. There is much to tell,' said the Vicious One. 'But we must move.'

It found the lingering scent of corruption and headed after the vehicles. After some hesitation, the Pious One followed, and then the rest of the team joined in.

# CHAPTER SIXTEEN

The hieroglyphics on the alien pillar flashed a series of colors Fiona had never seen before. Then the enormity of the object hit her.

"I need to sit down," she mumbled. She wobbled in place, and Ramecker redirected her to a chair. Fiona's chest tightened and her breaths came quick and shallow.

"Slow it down, slow it down," said Ramecker. "Long, deep breaths."

Fiona tried to listen, but the incessant pounding of her heart nauseated her. It was like the war all over again. It could not be possible, and yet it was right there in front of her. "I think I'm going to puke," she said as she rushed outside the building.

There was nothing in her stomach except a thick glob of bitter, yellow bile. She forced it out, letting the searing pain of acid in her throat bring her back to her senses. She stayed bent over, trying to spit out the last bits of the bile's flavor, until the shaking in her hands stopped.

Someone put their hand on her shoulder. Fiona stood up.

Cheung handed her some bottled water, and she used it to rinse her mouth. "I think we all had the same reaction," he said. He swayed side to side, and steadied himself against the door frame.

"Even you?"

"Worse. I had chili dogs for dinner."

Fiona smiled, took a deep, cleansing breath, and went back inside. The alien pillar was still there.

"So is Michael Davis an alien?" Fiona asked. It felt weird saying it out loud.

"No," said Cheung. "He's thoroughly human. But what I found out during my research was that he had a specific gene that coded for a protein that bonds to the zombie toxin. It changed the toxin. It still infected Davis, but he didn't show any symptoms."

"Like turning into an undead cannibal?" said Fiona. "How did you know it's alien?"

A bead of sweat dripped down Cheung's face, and his eyes had trouble concentrating on Fiona. "Wilcox had some . . . he had an epiphany. And I confirmed it with my research. It was a long process."

Lights danced in an unusual swirl across the alien pillar. Fiona tried to follow it with her eyes but just couldn't. She didn't think that Cheung gave the whole explanation, but she couldn't expect him to summarize ten years of research so quickly. "You weren't the only one to study the virus or toxin or whatever. Someone else would have noticed its nature and spoken about it."

"Yes, during the war, when the most scientists were researching the toxin, we weren't concerned with its nature. We just wanted a way to defeat it. And after the war, they all just disappeared."

"Killed? What about you?"

Cheung shrugged in answer to the first part of Fiona's question. "I was just too valuable for Wilcox."

Fiona didn't know what to make of what Cheung said. He experimented on Davis for nearly ten years, but he must have always had the greater good in mind. It was the only explanation for why he would do it. Fiona's thoughts and emotions felt like they could have gone through a blender. "If the zombie toxin is alien, what is its purpose?"

"That's a simple answer that Wilcox figured out right away. It's a weapon. Designed to destroy us."

"Destroy us?" Fiona's eyes widened. "Like dropping bombs on your enemy before . . ."

"Before an invasion. And that meteor shower the other night makes me think its already happening."

"But what does Wilcox want? He's with the military. He's the one who'll fight the aliens if there is an invasion." Fiona suddenly felt like she switched over to Wilcox's side. Long, deep breaths cleared her of her instantaneous nausea.

Cheung rubbed his chin. "That's the thing. I don't think he's really with the military. I mean, they give him his paycheck, but I think he answers to someone else. Things I've seen over the years. Things I've heard him say. And we've known about the aliens for years. Wilcox hasn't ordered any build up of forces or defenses. It's like he wants the invasion to happen.

"But one thing really bothered me, once I'd thought about it." Cheung moved in closer to Fiona, as if what he was about to say was for her only. "How did he know about Davis?"

"The guy can control zombies, that's how," Fiona blurted.

Cheung shook his head. "Davis told me he never used his abilities for that short bit of time he had after the war. And the old couple that rescued him after his zombie attack died. It was a secret. Davis was the only one who knew he had any control over the zombies. And yet, Wilcox knew Davis was infected."

Fiona wondered what Davis would have thought about all this. He was the center of a conspiracy he probably knew nothing about. Dr. Cheung and General Wilcox knew more about Davis than he knew about himself.

Ramecker tapped Cheung and Fiona on their shoulders. "Hey, I think there's an emergency." She led them outside the building, and the rest of Cheung's people followed.

In the west, a giant plume of smoke reached through the clouds. It stood starkly against the blue sky, as ominous and monolithic as the alien pillar in the building. It wasn't there earlier in the day, and achieving that size in a short time was too much for a wildfire.

"Is that Long Beach?" asked Fiona. "Are aliens attacking?"

"No, that fire's too far north," said Ramecker. She rested her hand on her gun's grip, as if she expected to draw it sometime soon. "It could be the military base."

"Or the refugee city," said Cheung. "Wherever it is, I doubt that it's a coincidence that it's happening right now."

They all stood in silence, staring at the distant conflagration. It was a strange silence, and Fiona could almost feel everyone's anxiousness in the air. They were a small group of people that knew that the fire was more than just a fire. It was the start of a new war.

Fiona remembered experiencing the same moment fifteen years ago, a moment of complete upheaval when the past meant nothing and the future meant death.

"What is that?" someone asked and pointed towards the horizon.

Fiona looked up and down the tower of smoke and noticed nothing unusual. She lowered her gaze and saw a different cloud. Dust billowing out from the desert floor and getting larger as it grew closer. "Those are vehicles," Fiona said. "They followed us."

"Impossible," said Ramecker. "I checked for tails."

Fiona felt her arm, prodding the sore injection sight. "They didn't have to follow us. They bugged me."

Cheung wobbled as the strength left his knees. Ramecker caught his arm before he fell. "Wilcox played me," he said. "He knew I would bring you here, Fiona. Somehow, he knew I had the alien technology."

Ramecker pushed Cheung into the building, and the doctor stumbled along with her. "We have to get out of here. We've got to get the technology away from Wilcox."

She pointed at the surrounding people. "Get out of here. Scatter."

After a brief, awkward pause, everyone else ran to their cars and drove off in all directions. The dust cloud in the distance widened as Wilcox's people spread out to follow the cars. Fiona ran inside the building with Ramecker and Cheung.

Cheung sat despondent on a chair while Ramecker rolled a large, flat trolley up to the alien pillar. She tossed a lasso around the pillar. "Help me with this," she said.

Fiona grabbed the end of the rope, and together she and Ramecker heaved at the pillar. Sweat broke out over Fiona's forehead, and the rope slowly ground its way into her palms. No matter how hard she strained, the pillar refused to move.

And then it pulled free, as if gravity somehow forgot the pillar existed. Fiona cringed, waiting for the pillar to crash down on the trolley. Instead, it landed gently, almost weightlessly. Ramecker and Fiona rolled the pillar out the back entrance of the building, and the object suddenly had mass again.

A pick-up truck waited next to a loading platform, and the pillar went in the truck's bed. Ramecker lashed the thing down, and pulled something out of the front seat of the truck. She handed a rifle to Fiona. "AK-47. You know how to use one?"

Fiona shook her head. "I used a bolt action during the war."

"Damn scientists. Here, learn fast." Ramecker gave Fiona the crash course and shoved a burlap bag full of loaded magazines into her hands. She ran inside and came back out half-dragging, half-carrying Cheung. She loaded him in the passenger seat.

Sand crunched behind Fiona, and she turned around to face a soldier coming around the corner of the building. Or at least, he moved like a trained soldier. He didn't wear a uniform. Fiona pulled the trigger on her weapon and hit everything except her target.

The soldier ducked out of the way, but never got back up. Ramecker pulled her pistol and blasted a few rounds through the man's chest, then put another one in his head just to be sure.

"Maybe I should drive," Fiona suggested.

"Do you know where to go?"

The rifle felt heavy in Fiona's hands. "No."

"Just don't forget to reload."

Fiona dropped her empty magazine and slapped a new one in place. Ramecker hopped into the driver's seat, and Fiona jumped into the back. The truck's wheels spun out, then the vehicle lurched as it took off into the desert.

Another soldier came around the building, and Fiona sent a more controlled blast his way. She didn't hit anything, and the truck drove out of range.

"To the left!" Ramecker shouted through the back window.

Two jeeps hurtled across the sand and gravel towards them. Fiona let off a burst and surprised herself when the bullets thunked into the sides of one of the jeeps. She pulled the trigger again, and the passenger in the jeep screamed out a rain of blood.

"Great shot," said Ramecker. Fiona wished she could say it was just like killing zombies, but it wasn't.

She shot again, shattering the windshield and destroying the driver. Then man slumped over, yanking the wheel hard and sending the vehicle tumbling until it broke apart in a tornado of heavy metal.

One of the passengers in the other jeep stood up through the roof and aimed his rifle at Fiona. She ducked behind the alien pillar just as bullets whizzed over head. Some smacked into the pillar, and the pillar gave out an electric hum that Fiona could feel more than hear.

The truck swung sideways, and Fiona had to grab on to the pillar so that she wouldn't get beat up by the sudden move. "Hang on," Ramecker said. Thanks for the warning, Fiona thought.

Ramecker slammed the side of the truck into the the jeep. Metal screeched as it scraped against metal, and the two vehicles whined as they tried to push each other out of their path.

The shooter on top whipped around with the impact, and he tried to right himself when Fiona emptied her weapon on him. The wind rushing over the jeep took away most of the bits of his head that broke loose while the rest spilled out over the roof of the vehicle.

The two vehicles separated a moment, and the man in the jeep's passenger seat tried to pull out his pistol. Fiona aimed at him, but her gun was empty. The man pointed his gun out the window at Ramecker's head.

Fiona brought her rifle down on his hand. His elbow caught against the window sill, and the limb bent backwards at the joint. Bone and muscle tore through the skin in a juicy explosion. Ramecker crashed the truck into the jeep again, catching the dangling arm between the two vehicles.

Ramecker pulled out her pistol and shot the driver once in the face. The driver grabbed his face to dam the river of blood, and the one-armed passenger tried to take over the wheel. The jeep separated from the truck and careened into a large boulder. The vehicle stopped instantly, but the two inside kept moving forward. The windshield grated them like cheese as they passed through, and the ground pulverized their bodies.

"There's another one," said Ramecker.

It was another truck. Three figures stood in the bed. Two of them concealed their faces with cloaks that flapped in the wind. The third was Wilcox.

Fiona reloaded and aimed at the driver. Her first shot hit him squarely in the chest, and his guts showered across the windshield, but the truck did not swerve. The driver wiped away his own gore from the window and picked up speed until they were right on Ramecker's tail.

One of Wilcox's companions crawled onto the roof of the truck and tossed off his cloak. It was a zombie, but not like anything Fiona had ever seen. It had claws and fangs and a face deformed with an overgrowth of veins. The thing hissed loudly enough for Fiona to hear over the desert wind and the roar of engines, then it leapt from its truck.

The distance was two great for a human to make, let alone a zombie, but as the monster reached the top of its arc, Fiona knew that it would land safely. She pulled the trigger. The zombie changed directions mid-air and crashed back down onto Wilcox's truck. The general reached over and pushed the body aside onto the ground.

The other person removed its cloak, and it was the same kind of zombie as the first. It made the leap, and Wilcox provided covering fire this time. Fiona had to take cover, and she heard the zombie land heavily on the pillar.

With its claws, it started slashing away at the ropes that held the pillar down. Lying on the floor, Fiona shot up at the zombie, but somehow the monster dodged her bullets. It swiped at her, sending her rifle flying over the edge of the truck. It continued cutting away at the pillar's bindings.

Fiona punched the zombie in the nuts so hard she thought she might have broken the zombie's bladder. The thing just looked at her and brought its claws down on her. She raised her arms to protect her self, but the claws felt as sharp as a surgeon's scalpel, and the intensity of the pain shocked the air out of her lungs.

The zombie stood over her, ready to eat her throat and drink her blood. A gun fired and pulped the zombie's knee. The monster took a step back, and the knee buckled backwards. The gun fired again, punching a hole through the zombie's neck. The tangle of facial veins drained of blood, and the zombie went limp. Fiona kicked it in the face, and it rolled out the back of the truck.

Cheung pointed the gun at Wilcox, but the general's truck stayed too far back. "How bad are you hurt?" he asked Fiona.

Fiona's arms looked like they lost a fight with an alligator. "It's not bad. I'll live."

"Look out!" Cheung started firing again, and Fiona could only duck down. The zombie came back over the edge of the truck, the last of its life spurting out of its neck. It grabbed the pillar and heaved. Despite the difficulty Fiona and Ramecker had moving the thing, the zombie pulled it out with ease.

Fiona reached out and grabbed the pillar, but the zombie was too strong. It slipped through her arms, and the alien technology slammed into the ground, squishing the zombie underneath. Wilcox's vehicle pulled up along side the pillar, and Ramecker accelerated the car away.

"Turn around!" yelled Cheung.

"We can't," said Ramecker. "Wilcox's other men wouldn't have been too far behind. It's lost."

Cheung's head drooped.

"It's not entirely lost," said Fiona. Cheung looked back, and Ramecker checked her rearview mirror.

Fiona held up the smooth crystal, separated from the pillar.

# Chapter Seventeen

The ashes from the fire came down softly, like snow in the middle of summer. It was so peaceful Halley didn't even notice the blazing heat pouring out from the city.

Every step Jacey took sent up a billowing cloud of the ash. He was pretty sure her name was Jacey. Halley, however, dragged his feet. The charcoal crust over his stump had started to flake off, revealing little rivers of red like lava underneath cooled earth. The pain in his arm burned like lava, too. The injury reeked of steak and gasoline, and every whiff made Halley want to faint. The only thing he could do to stay conscious was to follow Jacey wherever she led him.

"Where are we going?" he mumbled. He said it again when he realized Jacey didn't hear him.

"To the front of the city. There might be merchants outside watching the fire. Maybe we can hitch a ride with one of them."

"Why would any of the merchants be outside. There's a huge fire right here."

"It's a disaster. Wherever there's a disaster, people will be watching."

Halley tried to catch up to Jacey to make the conversation easier, but it seemed as if his strength leaked out of his wound just like the blood and other fluids. "You don't look too sad. Isn't this city your home?"

"This place was never my home. I have no one. But it still hurts to see it burn. And all those people." Her voice trailed off.

Halley slowed his pace to put more distance between him and Jacey. "You know I was the one to set fire to the city, right?"

She didn't respond.

"Why didn't you let Davis kill me? If you knew our history, you would've let him kill me."

"It's just the way it is."

What a strange person, Halley thought. How could she have survived a life in the refugee city with that attitude? Early in the war, Halley learned that killing your problems, zombie or human, was the best way to make it to the next morning. And maybe the war was over, but that didn't mean that lessons learned in the war were wrong.

They reached the front of the city and headed towards the city gate. There were several trucks and jeeps in front, and Halley's helicopter fleet was grounded. A group of soldiers and civilians sat in a circle, and another, smaller group of civilians stood around them.

Jacey tried to get under Halley's good arm to help him walk. "Come on, let's go."

He pulled her behind a large growth of chaparral. "I don't think it's safe."

"What do you mean? Aren't you one of them?"

Halley pointed through the leaves.

Everyone sitting down, military or otherwise, was a prisoner. Those standing up wore no uniforms and carried small machine pistols. Mercenaries, maybe? One of them conversed on a walkie-talkie, and when he was finished, he relayed his information to a cloaked figure.

"That's a gangster. From inside the city," said Jacey. Halley nodded.

The cloaked figure brushed its hand through the air, as if it did not want to waste words. The rest of the mercenaries joined up in a bunch and opened fire on the sitting people.

The mass of bullets was so great that even completely ruined bodies still danced to the impact like broken scarecrows in the wind. Still, some of the prisoners managed to scramble to their feet and make a break for it. Few got very far before a mercenary took them down.

One person ran straight towards Halley's and Jacey's hiding spot. A mercenary took aim and shot the runner in the face. A chunk of his head burst away, but he kept running. With every step, his dangling eyeball would alternate between slapping his jaw or slapping his forehead. Another shot rang out, and his intestines drenched the plant that concealed Halley. The man stumbled then died, falling onto the bush. The branches held his body up, so that he looked like he'd been caught in a spider's web. Jacey curled herself as small as possible to avoid the brains dripping out of the broken eye socket.

A mercenary walked up and dragged the body off the bush and tossed it to the ground. Instead of wasting bullets, he stomped on the head until nothing was left. He started to leave, and then he turned around.

Did he hear something? Halley tried to make himself smaller without disturbing the bushes. His stump scraped across the sharp end of a twig. He bit his lip until a thin trickle of blood came out, but it wasn't enough. He let out a small whimper.

The mercenary popped around the bush, weapon raised. He motioned to Halley and Jacey to get up. Jacey rose quickly, but with one arm, Halley had some difficulty. At gun point, the mercenary led them to the rest of the group.

Someone went through the bodies, putting a bullet into each one, including the ones that didn't move anymore. Halley remembered doing the exact same thing to zombies during the war. Even humans, just in case they got any ideas about coming back from the dead.

One of the mercenaries stepped forward. He looked like more of a cruel bastard than all his friends, if that was possible. "You're Halley, right? Major Thomas Halley?" He looked over at the pile of dead bodies. "Your pilots told us that you went down."

Halley waved his stump around. "I didn't do this for fun. Do I know you?"

"You can call me Rex." He pointed at three of his men. "Find whatever hole he crawled out of and make sure nothing else comes out.

The cloaked figure stood next to Rex and whispered something in his ear. Halley couldn't see the face under the hood clearly, but it was deformed somehow.

Rex turned back to Halley. "General Wilcox may need to talk to you. You really messed everything up, man. This girl, on the other hand, is useless."

A mercenary forced Jacey onto her knees, and Rex drew a pistol and put it against her head. Jacey was too shocked to even cry out.

Shit, thought Halley, they're going to kill her. "She's a friend of Michael Davis."

Rex hesitated for a second then raised his weapon. He looked at the cloaked figure, and it shook its head. "It's your lucky day, girl."

The mercenaries bound Jacey's hands, tied Halley's hand to his leg, and herded them into a truck. Rex sat with them, the barrel of his gun always pointing at one or the other.

In between the pulses of pain coming from his lost arm, Halley found it interesting that he bothered to save Jacey's life. Even Davis tried to save the girl's life. Did they see something in her that maybe they lost a long time ago? Halley decided he'd rather focus on his pain. He didn't enjoy introspection.

They drove not back towards the base, but east, away from most civilized areas. They left the former Los Angeles County when Wilcox met them. He rode at the head of his own entourage of vehicles coming from the opposite direction. The vehicles were covered in dust, and some looked recently banged up. One large truck carried a small group of prisoners, most with bloody noses or busted jaws, and another truck carried a large, long piece of stone.

The two groups stopped in the middle of the road. Wilcox got out first, followed by his men. Halley guessed that they were mercenaries, just like the ones that held him and Jacey captive. Wilcox's driver got out next. He also wore a long cloak that concealed his face, and he had a gaping wound in the middle of his chest. It didn't seem to bother him.

Rex dragged Halley out and dropped him in front of Wilcox. Without the use of his remaining arm, Halley lost his balance and fell to his knees. Wilcox stood over him, glared down at him like some kind of medieval executioner.

"What the hell happened here?" Wilcox asked. He tapped Halley's stump with a booted foot. Crumbs of black crust dislodged, releasing a small trickle of blood. Halley ground his teeth and shot his breath out in a long hiss to stop himself from passing out. "I told you to kill the alien, but you torched the city. I could cover up the first. People are going to ask questions about the second."

"Zombies," Halley said through the spasms of pain in his stump.

Wilcox knelt down and got close to Halley. "What did you say?"

"Zombies. There were zombies in the city. I had to kill them."

The general cocked his head, contemplating what Halley just said. He stood up. "Is this true? You released zombies?"

The cloaked figure that came with Rex spoke. "It was necessary. We lost control of the creature. If it escaped, it could have alerted the rest of its kind to our presence."

"Zombies eat people," Wilcox said, almost growling. "We want to control them, not make them dinner. If there's another outbreak . . ."

"It is inconsequential. Your pathetic species means nothing on the grand scale of the universe. What matters is that the invasion happens." It removed its cloak, revealing its nightmarish, deformed body. It pointed at itself. "This human flesh is not even strong enough to hold the gift within it."

Halley forgot his pain. The creature before him was shaped like a man, but it was a monster to behold. It chilled him to see it, and its presence was more unbelievable than that of an alien.

Wilcox stepped towards the monster, studying the tangle of veins on its face. "What haven't you told me. What are you hiding?"

The monster gave Wilcox a toothy grin. "We told you everything you needed to know to do your job. What are you hiding from us? Michael Davis perhaps?"

Wilcox raised his eyebrows.

"Many years ago you said he was dead," said the monster. "Have you been experimenting behind our backs?"

The sun beat down on the gathering of humans and inhumans, slowly roasting the ground so that the air felt like it was ejected from a furnace. A soft breeze whispered by. It did nothing to tame the heat, but it brought with it the faint scent of a burning city from miles away. Wilcox and the monster held each other's gaze.

Faster than Halley's eyes could see, claws flashed towards Wilcox's throat. Halley expected to see the general's head go flying, but Wilcox caught the monster's arm before it could reach him. He cranked the arm, putting all his strength into it. The strain forced the veins on his neck to bulge out. They crawled up Wilcox's neck and onto his face until they were thick as ropes and pulsating with blood.

The other monster ran up behind Wilcox, tossing off its cloak as it ran. The general shoved away his captive and wheeled around to face the other monster. He forced his fist through the wound in the monster's chest, and his other hand stabbed the monster's eyes. He lifted the monster up and brought it's neck down on his knee. The bones cracked as loud as a gunshot, and the body went limp.

The first monster shook the pain out of its arm and charged at Wilcox, slashing with its claws. Wilcox dodged every attack and clawed with his normal hands when he had the chance. His nails caught the monster's face veins, and the meat ripped apart like wet tissue.

Blood blinding its eyes, the monster retreated from Wilcox. The general forced the monster to the ground, and he coiled his arms around its neck. He squeezed until the monster's eyes bugged out from its head and the flow of blood to its ruptured veins stopped. The spine broke with the crunch of wet gravel.

Wilcox stood, breathing deep. The veins on his face shrunk until he was again human. "Who's next?"

Rex raised his hands, and the rest of his men followed suit.

"Good," said Wilcox. Monster gore dripped from his face and hands. "We've been betrayed, and it's time to set things right."

# CHAPTER EIGHTEEN

A thick blanket of hot ash reached from wall to wall in the refugee city. The entire landscape was flat except for the occasional melted steel beam that stuck up like a dead tree in the desert. Wind whipped through, kicking up the ash in little twisters and sending the particles out beyond the wall, slowly erasing away the refugee city. Davis wondered if this is what the end of the world looked like.

When the fire reached its most hellish point, Davis found safety. It was a basement with walls of solid concrete and a strong ceiling. He found some rags to make bandages for his zombie wounds, and caring for himself took his mind off of the roaring inferno above. The heat rose to a point were Davis wasn't sure if it was zombie poison in his veins giving him a fever or if it was the fire cooking him alive. But it eventually died down, and Davis crawled out of the basement.

He stepped out into the moon, its light shining as white as the ashes underneath it. There were other groups of survivors coming out of whatever hole they used as safety. Davis guessed there couldn't be more than a hundred survivors. They wandered around aimlessly. Since the war, the refugee city had been their home, and now only the walls remained.

On the far side of the city, the large gates opened, and everyone headed in that direction. Davis headed in that direction, too. He had nothing else to do.

The gate was roughly half a mile away, and Davis couldn't see anything clearly, but he did make out the shape of a large truck or jeep driving through the gate. People ran towards it, and a stuttering flash of fire came out of the top of the vehicle. Moments later, the staccato of gun fire echoed across the empty city.

People fled, but the vehicle gave pursuit, and more came in from the outside to join in the hunt. They shot the survivors down when they were far away, or they just crushed them beneath their tires when they felt like it.

Davis jumped under a pile of rubble and tossed ash across his body and face for camouflage. Around him, he heard the roar of engines, followed by the boom of the guns and the screams of death. Davis didn't know how long it went on, but the shooters didn't seem to be in a hurry.

Eventually, the shooting slowed down and the time between screams lengthened. A truck stopped near Davis's hiding place, and Davis wormed his way deeper in. Two men jumped out of the truck and spread out to look for survivors.

Chunks of wood still glowed orange inside of Davis's burrow. A piece of rebar stuck out of the embers, and Davis ripped off a piece of his shirt sleeve to wrap a handle around the steel. Then he waited for the men to return to their truck, and when they did, he pulled his weapon out of the fire and scrambled out of his hole.

The molten tip of his weapon easily burned a hole through the first man's back and came out the other side sizzling. He pulled out the rebar and swatted it at the other's head. His brow bones caved in and the rebar stopped halfway through his brain.

Making sure to keep out of site of the other vehicles driving around, Davis switched his clothes for those worn by the second man. He expected them to be Wilcox's men and wear uniforms, but they looked more like hired guns. He took the car keys and rolled the bodies into his hiding spot, tossing some ash on top of them for good measure.

The gunfire and the screaming continued. Davis wished he could block it out, but the pain in the dying voices was too strong. In his years in his cell, he learned the depths that Wilcox and Halley and even Cheung could descend into, but he forgot that there were more people like them in the world.

A weak burst of laughter brought Davis to attention. He spun around looking for the source, but the laughter came again from a different direction. Then another direction. And then another.

There was no laughter, but it squirmed through Davis's head nonetheless. And it only sounded like laughter, but it was an imitation, as if it were made by something that had no concept of humor. Something that wasn't human at all.

Davis kicked through the ashes following the growing strength of the laughter to locate the source. Underneath a blackened piece of corrugated steel, Davis found a shattered piece of a monster's skull.

'You are throwing away your chance for greatness,' the skull said into his mind. The voice faded in and out, like a weak radio signal. Davis imagined that after getting crushed and burned, there couldn't be much life left in the skull. Or un-life.

'We have survived for countless generations,' the skull continued. 'We survived so many generations traveling among so many stars. Your primitive minds would not remain sane if it could comprehend our journeys. And all the while we were hunted and persecuted, but we survived.

'Even now, when all that remains of my kin are brittle bones clinging to life beyond death, we have plans to survive.

'You will have choices to make. The survival of your species depends on the survival of mine. Follow the woman. The one from your past. You will understand.'

Davis didn't know what to make of it. But the thing mentioned Elise. She survived the fire. Of course she survived the fire.

He waited for the skull to say more, but it remained silent. He ground the piece underfoot and gave it a few extra stomps just to ensure the thing stayed dead. He headed to his new truck and jumped in. He started it up and listened to the engine rumble.

It had been awhile since he last drove a car. He hoped it was like riding a bike. The truck's tank was full, and Davis could take that as far as it lasted. Then he could hitch hike or walk as far as that could take him.

But Elise was out there. She was the only one that could tell him the truth. And the zombies she controlled turned their victims instantly. Did she have more of them outside the refugee city? No matter how far Davis ran, the zombies would always catch up.

And what about Jacey? He still owed her a favor. She was probably dead, killed by these same people who killed the survivors of the fire. He hardly knew her, but he did know that she was a good person. She didn't deserve a life in the refugee city, and she didn't deserve a death at the hands of these scumbags. Davis figured he owed her an even bigger favor now.

He drove towards the city gate, moving slowly so that the billowing ash didn't block his view. He drove through and slowed his vehicle. In front of him was the open road. To his right, there were four men guarding the entrance to the city. They sat around a campfire playing cards. The rest of the trucks were still in the city. They couldn't catch up to him. All he had to do was push his foot down on the accelerator. Then he would be free.

But that wouldn't be true. He lost his freedom that day in the forest when Elise left him to die. The moment the zombies tore into his flesh and infected him with their disease, he had no freedom. He wasn't the same person. He wasn't even sure he was human. And without his memory, the only person he knew as Michael Davis was the one with the scars on his body and zombie blood in his veins. He was a prisoner within himself.

Davis turned off the truck's engine and hopped out. He grabbed one of the several rifles stashed inside and headed for the group playing cards.

One of them looked up at him. "You want us to deal you in on the next hand?"

"Don't bother," said Davis. He shoved the barrel of the rifle into the man's eye and pulled the trigger. Slivers of skull and pink lumps of brain blossomed out of the back of the man's head and plastered the other three. Some pieces landed in the camp fire and started to fry.

One man went for his rifle on the ground. Davis kicked him so hard in the jaw that the bone split right down the middle, and as the man fell on his back, gravity pulled the two pieces open on either side of his head.

The other two could barely scramble to their feet before Davis cut them down. He gathered up their weapons and tossed them into the back of his truck. The other men inside the city heard the commotion and started for the city gates.

Davis hopped up into the back of his truck and manned the machine gun. It was a big .50 caliber, and it was conveniently ready for him to use. He pointed the gun at the other trucks. They probably didn't expect one of their own to open fire on them.

He pushed down on the trigger, and the force exploding out of the gun rattled through him like an earthquake. The first truck went down easily, and Davis pivoted to direct his continuous stream of gunfire at the other trucks. Soon, all the vehicles were dead.

The surviving men hobbled out, some of them missing limbs, and tried to man their own guns. Davis kept shooting until he was empty then chose one of the rifles at his feet.

Back in that forest, Davis was the one with the rifle aimed at Wolff. Maybe he had a special skill? There was only one way to find out. Davis brought up his weapon, lining the sights up with one of the distant men. One by one he picked them off. He didn't feel like checking to make sure they were all dead. That they were down was enough for him.

He started up his truck and headed down the highway. It felt like he just made the first of the choices that alien skull told him about.

# CHAPTER NINETEEN

Ramecker slid the tip of her pocket knife into Fiona's shoulder. Fiona bit down hard on the wad of cloth between her teeth and dug her nails into her thighs. The blade wormed around in Fiona's arm, and the pain transformed into nausea.

"I can feel it," said Ramecker.

The edge of Fiona's vision started to go black.

"Got it." Ramecker pulled out what looked like a tiny glass pill. "Yup, it's a tracking device." She crushed it between two rocks.

Ramecker wrapped up Fiona's shoulder, and with the bandages around the slashes on her arms, Fiona felt like a mummy. "Wilcox won't be able to follow us?"

"I don't think he'll be able to follow us, but that doesn't mean he won't come looking for us. Do you think he saw you take the crystal off of the pillar?"

Fiona shook her head. "He stopped once he got the pillar. He's never seen it, so maybe he doesn't know it's not complete."

They were in an oasis, a forest of palm trees, with only the moon and their truck's headlights for illumination. The alien crystal rested on the ground, and Cheung paced around it, variously looking at it or the sky, as if he expected a second one to fall out of space. Even in the moonlight, the crystal appeared dull and mundane.

Cheung stopped in his tracks and turned to the two women. His eyes were wild with fever, and his voice strained to be heard. "Did you notice how the pillar reacted around the zombie?"

Fiona's arms throbbed. "I was a little distracted."

"The lights on the pillar. They flashed in a pattern I hadn't observed before. And the crystal glowed differently. I think that the zombie activated it somehow."

"You mean the zombie powered it up?" Fiona asked.

Cheung shook his head vigorously. "The only difference between us and the zombies is that the zombies are infected with alien genes. I think the pillar read the genetic material, the way we would do a fingerprint or retinal scan."

"So what does this knowledge give us?" asked Ramecker. "Don't let zombies near the pillar? Wilcox has tons of those things locked up in storage."

"It's not the zombies," said Cheung. He leaned in close, almost as if he were afraid someone else was listening. "It's the alien's genes. If an alien got near it, it would unlock the pillar's potential."

"And maybe the pillar doesn't work without the crystal," suggested Fiona. "Maybe it's a power source for the rest of the thing."

Ramecker pulled her pistol from its holster. "Then I say we destroy it."

Cheung threw himself between the crystal and the gun. "No!" he screamed with almost too much earnestness.

"Doctor," Ramecker said. "Get out of the way."

Fiona stared at the two, frozen in her spot. She didn't even know whose side she was on.

"This is an important scientific artifact," said Cheung. He knelt down and scooped up the crystal, cradling it like a baby. Faint light shimmered in the heart of the crystal. "We have to figure out what it does. What knowledge it holds."

"It's not just some curiosity any more." Ramecker continued pointing her gun even though Cheung held the crystal. "Wilcox came after the thing. It's essential to whatever his plan is."

Fiona knew something bad was going to happen. She could feel it in her gut. Ramecker was right that Wilcox needed the crystal to fulfill whatever plans he had. They had to keep the thing out of his hands. But to destroy the crystal? Ramecker was a fighter, not a scientist like Fiona and Cheung. She didn't look far enough into the future to see why the crystal had to be preserved. If they could figure out what technology the crystal held, they could reverse the damage caused by the war and even advance scientific knowledge by centuries or millennia.

"I'm going to count to three," said Ramecker.

"And then what?" asked Cheung half-mockingly.

"One."

Fiona looked between the crystal and the gun. If what Cheung said earlier in the day was right, Wilcox wanted an alien invasion. Another war. So many died fighting against the zombies, but how many more would die fighting against creatures from another world? They already infected Earth with a zombie plague; they didn't care about the survival of humanity.

"Two."

Fiona's hands rummaged across the ground, stopping when they found a fist-sized rock. She flung the stone, hitting Ramecker in the temple.

Her eyes went blank and a thin stream of blood spurted out of her head. She dropped her gun and stumbled backwards, tripping over a dead palm frond. Cheung gently rolled the crystal away from him and picked up the gun.

"On your knees," he said. Ramecker looked dazed, but she still obeyed.

Now Fiona stepped in front of the gun. "You can't kill her."

"She's working against us."

"She's one of us."

Cheung waved the gun around wildly then regained his composure. His hand shook as he held the gun to Ramecker, and sweat dripped down his forehead and flowed across his nose. "Dammit," he said and lowered the gun. "Tie her up."

Ramecker shifted a little and looked ready to spring to her feet. Cheung blasted several bullets into the ground not more than a foot in front of Ramecker. Sand kicked up, and Ramecker fell backwards and stayed on the ground.

The truck was well stocked with survival gear, including a length of rope. Fiona grabbed it and started wrapping it around Ramecker's wrists and ankles.

"He's going mad," said Ramecker, her whisper low enough that Cheung couldn't hear.

"There's something special about the alien pillar," said Fiona. "Why else would Wilcox want it? It's too important to destroy."

"It's too important to not destroy."

Cheung grabbed the crystal again. He held it under one arm, and with the other, he pointed the gun at both Fiona and Ramecker. "All right, hurry up. Get her in the back of the truck."

To Fiona, the gun looked even more dangerous with it pointed in her direction. Only when Cheung stepped away did she feel safe enough to move. She helped Ramecker to hop towards the truck, then she pushed her in the bed and closed the tail gate.

"You're driving," said Cheung. It sounded more like an order than a request.

Once they were back on the road, Fiona asked "Where are we going?"

The front of Cheung's shirt was drenched in sweat, and his eyes wavered, as if they couldn't focus on anything. The gun rested loosely in his hand. "Back to Los Angeles. The lab."

"Won't that make it easier for Wilcox to find us?"

"It doesn't matter!" Cheung snapped. His grip tightened on the gun, and his roving eyes stopped on Fiona. She risked a look and saw the slow hemorrhage of red over the whites of his eyes. A thin stream of drool flowed out from between his teeth and puddled on the top of his gun. "Just keep driving."

The crystal sat in Cheung's lap. He had been the one to hold onto the object the longest, and Fiona wondered if something was leeching out of it and into Cheung. "Doctor, are you . . . well?"

"No," he said with a little chuckle. "I've been poisoned. I guess the symptoms are starting to show, aren't they?"

Fiona kept her eyes on the road. With every passing moment, Cheung became stranger, as if a fever was boiling his brain. "Is it the crystal? Does it have some kind of alien radioactivity?"

"Don't be an idiot. It was Wilcox. He tricked me. Double-crossed me. He took it all for himself." He spoke like a man possessed.

Fiona thought that if she kept Cheung talking, he'd forget about the gun in his hand. "What did he take?"

"My research. It was for both of us. But he poisoned me."

"What did he poison you with?"

"My research."

It took a moment for the meaning behind Cheung's words to sink into Fiona's head. She felt a spasm in her gut, as if a black hole sucked everything in. To stop the chattering of her teeth, she had to clench her jaw until the muscles in her head burned. Out of the corner of her eye, she caught another thick line of spit fall out of Cheung's mouth. He was like a hungry wolf.

The miles passed, and Cheung's breathing became progressively more harsh. Fiona thought he might have been dying, but everything else about him became stronger. He sat up straighter, and his red eyes stared down the road without any deviation.

The desert disappeared behind them, and outside the window, Fiona could see the little farms people made in empty lots and the lights in their homes.

"Do you think that the crystal will provide some kind of cure?" Fiona asked.

"There is no cure," Cheung whispered. "I don't want a cure. I want power. More power than Wilcox could imagine."

No cure. Without a doubt, this was not the Dr. Cheung that Fiona knew from long ago. In his ten years working with Wilcox and Halley, the goodness that was once in him died, replaced with some mad desire for domination over things he could never understand. And Fiona knew it wasn't the poison floating around in his veins that made him act strangely. It was all a choice. He and Wilcox couldn't let the war die. It was their moment of glory, and they were trying to bring it back. Fiona didn't want it to be real, but any of the illusions she believed were gone now.

Since the end of the war, she only wanted to do the right thing. And she failed.

The glass behind Fiona's head shattered, and Ramecker's booted foot smashed away the remaining shards. Ramecker reached through the window, rope still hanging off of one wrist, and chopped Cheung in the throat. A thick wad of phlegm flew out of his mouth, and he grabbed his neck while trying to suck in fresh air.

Ramecker boxed Fiona in the ear, then wound up and let her fist fly into Fiona's jaw. Fiona's head rebounded off the window, and the truck swerved before coming to a halt on the road's shoulder.

Blood trickled out of both sides of Fiona's head, and she had to wait for full consciousness to return. Ramecker wasn't in the back, and the passenger seat was empty, save for the alien crystal.

Ramecker had a ten yard head start, but Cheung had a gun. Despite his fervent state of mind, he steadily held up the gun and pulled the trigger. Ramecker fell and disappeared between rows of crops. Cheung rushed over to the spot. Fiona expected him to use the gun to finish Ramecker off, but instead he lunged on her like a lion on its prey.

A lot of time passed since the last time Fiona killed a zombie, but she didn't forget how it was done. She got out of the truck and found a nice stick she could use as a club. Ramecker's flesh squished loudly as Cheung tore off pieces and scarfed them down. Fiona hoped he was too distracted to notice her creeping up behind him.

Fiona was feet away when four men emerged from the darkness. Farmers, probably the land owners. "What the hell is going on here?" one of them asked. He held a shotgun resting on his shoulder.

Cheung stood up, blood soaking his arms from the hands to the shoulders. He didn't wait for the farmers to react to his presence. He leapt upon the nearest one and snapped his teeth into the man's throat. The other three backed away, pointing their guns but not shooting, too afraid to hit their friend.

Then, to Fiona's surprise, Ramecker stood up. What remained of her face slipped off her skull to reveal an unblinking monster. She jumped on the next farmer, bringing him to the ground.

Fiona backed away, slowly at first, then at a run. It shouldn't have been possible. Ramecker couldn't turn that quickly. And if the two farmers turn that fast too, Fiona would be quickly outnumbered. She returned to the truck, and behind her, she heard the farmers scream.

She jumped back in the truck and reversed to get it back onto the road. She looked outside the window one last time. Cheung walked towards her, his gait as normal as a person on a Sunday stroll. The only thing unusual about him was the gore hanging out of his mouth and the gun in his hand.

The truck kicked up a shower of sand as Fiona floored it. Cheung flew up onto the hood of the truck and smashed his face open on the windshield. Strands of his face stuck in the cracks of the glass, and Cheung peeled himself away.

Fiona slammed on the brakes, sending her old mentor flying. His bones snapped as he tumbled through the dirt, and blobs of blood exploded out of ruptures in his body. Fiona jumped out of the truck and grabbed Cheung's gun off of the ground. A lifetime of mistakes ends now, she told herself.

She emptied the gun to make sure nothing remained of the zombie's head. Ramecker and the farmers stumbled towards Fiona. She tossed the gun, wishing she had enough ammo to put them out of her misery. Before they could reach her, she got into the truck and jetted off into the night.

Before too many miles passed, she decided she needed to do something to stop the war.

# CHAPTER TWENTY

Davis found a place suitably far away from the military base and stopped his vehicle. He didn't think it would do him any good to drive up with a giant machine gun sticking out of the back of his truck. Most of his weapons were also too conspicuous to carry around, so he just took a knife and a small revolver.

Being locked up in a cell for years didn't do much to help Davis get familiar with the lay of the land, so he took his time getting to the base, sticking to the shadows and freezing at even the slightest hint that he might get caught. The bright moonlight helped him to find his path, but the bright lights and megaphone-amplified voices in the distance guided him even more. Something was going down.

Back in the refugee city, Jacey mentioned that the gangsters were allowed free passage in and out of the city.

If the soldiers there knew about it, it was guaranteed that Wilcox knew about it. Wilcox wasn't the kind of guy who would let them operate without some kind of back-up plan in case things went bad. There had to be information that Davis could use to find Elise.

Approaching the little enclave of civilian homes and businesses surrounding the base, Davis didn't know how suspicious he would look walking around in the middle of the night. But the town was in even more of an uproar than what he was able to tell from a distance. Most people were loading up their cars with foodstuffs and weapons, and some were going from building to building and looting anything that they found useful.

It had to be the fire. Everyone must have seen it and came to the same conclusion. The military purged the refugee city after an outbreak of zombies, which, to Davis's morbid amusement, was actually correct. A high concentration of people in an area was vulnerable to an infestation, and everyone was making their way to rural parts.

Soldiers policed the streets, but their enthusiasm suggested that they were just as anxious to leave as the civilians. Davis weaved his way through the crowds and chaos and walked onto the base without any hassle.

It was dark, and the last time Davis saw the base was almost ten years ago from the inside of a cage Halley had stuffed him in. But the few soldiers he saw could have been deserters based on the panic in their steps and the worry on their faces. These weren't Wilcox's people, sycophants like Halley. They were normal, trying to do a job, and they probably had families that ranked higher in importance than fighting another war against the undead.

But one person walking around wasn't a soldier. It was Dr. Todd. She carried a large rock, and she looked like she just got off a tour of the inside of a meat grinder. Davis walked up slowly, trying not to spook her. He didn't know what kind of guns she carried or what state her mind was in.

"Doctor," he said.

Todd yelped and dropped her rock. Despite the size of the thing, the stone bounced like a basketball. She twirled around and held up her hands, ready for a fight.

"It's me. Michael Davis."

It took a moment for her to realize who he was. "You escaped. How did you do it?"

"That doesn't matter. I think I need your help."

She picked up her rock and held it close to her chest. "I'm . . . I'm sorry, but I can't help." She leaned in closer, like she was about to divulge a secret. "Outside in the world, not in your lab, the zombies are back. And it might be my fault."

Davis laughed and shook his head. "No, it was Wilcox. Him and some friends of his."

Dr. Todd considered Davis's request for a moment. "Maybe we can help each other." They searched the base without any interference from passing soldiers. Along the way, Dr. Todd asked "What are you looking for?"

"I'm not sure," said Davis. "I need to find someone. Wilcox may have information that'll help me." He looked at Dr. Todd. She held her rock carefully, as if it were an atomic bomb. "What is that rock?"

"It's a crystal. It's for . . . I don't know what it's for. And you wouldn't believe me if I told you." She ended the conversation when she stopped in front of Wilcox's office.

Davis drew his revolver. "I'll go in first." The door swung open lightly, and Davis stormed in, finger ready to pull the trigger. The office was empty. He flicked the lights on and pulled Dr. Todd in, forgetting about the bandages on her arms. "Look for anything about gangsters or the refugee city."

"Anything specific?" A little bit of blood soaked through the bandages, and she rubbed her arms.

Davis shook his head. "Maybe payments received or shipments of machinery or whatever. They were well-equipped. Wilcox had to know something."

Dr. Todd set her crystal down on Wilcox's chair and started rummaging through file cabinets. She moved fast, ignoring most of what she saw. Davis went through the desk, but most of what he found was office supplies and memos dealing with the day-to-day activities of running the base.

"Look through this stuff," Dr. Todd said, dropping a massive packet of papers on the desk. They were invoices from the port of Long Beach.

Davis riffled through a few files. "Looks like Wilcox has been doing some business at the port. He must have been using his authority to import or export stuff for Elise."

"Elise?" Dr. Todd looked confused.

"It's a long story," said Davis. "Or at least its longer than what I told you before." He found information about a ship and the port that reappeared several times across the documents and remembered it. "We should get going, unless there's something you were looking for."

She didn't answer. Instead, she stared past Davis and back outside the office. Carefully, Davis pulled his revolver and kept it hidden against his body. He spun around, and the muzzle of his gun was mere inches away from the muzzle of a rifle.

A soft-eyed kid, his boots barely broken in, held them at gunpoint. The sheen of sweat glistened on his face, and the tip of his rifle wavered as he tried to conceal his nervousness. "Drop your gun. Get on your knees."

Dr. Todd obeyed, but Davis ignored him. The kid tried to put on a menacing face, but to Davis it looked like he was trying to pass some mean gas. Davis could've grabbed the kids rifle and put six rounds in his face at any moment he wanted.

"Put down the gun," said the kid.

"Just listen to him," said Dr. Todd.

Davis spoke to both of them. "No."

The kid tried again to threaten Davis.

Davis took in a deep breath and let it out slowly. "Do you know what's happening out there? It's starting again. The war. Do you remember the war?"

The kid shook his head. "I was too young."

"So you never had to kill anything?"

Again, the kid shook his head.

"Let me tell you something," Davis said. "There's a lot of killing that has to be done during war. But save it for the zombies. When you cross that line to killing humans, there's no turning back."

The kid's eyes flicked between Davis and Dr. Todd. The tip of the rifle started to drop, and then it came back up. Davis moved with lightning efficiency, grabbing the barrel of the rifle and pushing it towards the sky while a stream of bullets blasted through the ceiling. A heavy shove forced the kid into the wall behind him, and Davis forced his revolver into the kid's mouth, chipping a tooth in the process. He slowly pulled back on the hammer while tears started to pour down the kid's face. Dr. Todd stood up, but didn't dare interfere.

A simple pull of the trigger would make the problem disappear. "You really don't get it, do you?" Davis asked. "This is the end. A new war is starting. I could kill you right now and prevent you from suffering the way the two of us have suffered. But I'm trying to give you a chance to live and fight. Maybe you'll come out the other side."

The kid nodded, and Davis pulled out his gun and uncocked it. He tried to hand his rifle over to Davis, but the other shook his head.

"You'll need it. Get out of here."

With stumbling steps, the kid headed away. He looked ready to pass out.

"Hey, kid," Davis shouted. The kid paused and turned around. "Just FYI, there's also an alien invasion."

The expression on the kid's face went sour, and based on the bow-legged steps he took afterwards, Davis thought the kid shit his pants. He chuckled as he headed back into Wilcox's office.

"What do you mean, 'alien invasion?'" asked Dr. Todd.

Davis shrugged. "Exactly what I said. I know it's unbelievable, but I saw them. One of them even talked to me. In my head at least." To his surprise, Dr. Todd didn't seem too distressed.

She held up her crystal. "This belongs to them. It's one part of some kind of alien technology. I think Wilcox wanted to reverse engineer it or something."

"What does it do?"

Dr. Todd shook her head.

The thing was alien, and Wilcox was looking for it. Which probably meant that Elise wanted it, too. Davis knew the best course of action would be to destroy it, if that were possible. Then there would be no possibility of humans or aliens getting their hands on it. No worries, no stress. This was another choice Davis had to make.

"Okay, what do you need?" Davis asked. "What did you come here for?"

"The zombies. We need some way to stop them. I was thinking of Dr. Cheung's weapon."

Davis nodded. "There was always some in the lab, just in case."

"Can you go back there?"

"Yeah, it's like going back home."

# Chapter Twenty-One

The corruption hung heavy in the air, and the team followed the trail easily. But it hung even heavier inside the Vicious One. The body did what it could to defeat the infection, but after every successful attempt, the plague would reinvent itself and strike back harder. Only time stood between the Vicious One and the total corruption of its body.

The rest of the team knew that their leader would be gone soon. They stood far apart from the Vicious One, and only the Pious One looked as if it did not feel fear. But the Vicious One sensed that the Pious One had the greatest amount of fear. It owed the Vicious One its life, and it was likely unsure if it would be giving it to a pure being or a corrupted monster.

They tracked the Others far from the burning prison, and towards a large concentration of population.

The lights from the humans' dwellings went up into the night sky and outshone the stars. The Vicious One wondered if the human woman intended to detonate the bomb within the population of humans. What purpose would that serve?

As they entered the city, the Vicious One and its team took to the rooftops to minimize the chance that they would be seen. The Vicious One knew it was a useless gesture. They would have to engage the Others in combat soon enough, and that could not be hidden.

The Others' vehicles led them to the edge of the continent where the ocean met the land. It was some kind of industrial area that seemed to be used for the loading and unloading of cargo to or from overseas. It amazed the Vicious One that humans used such a primitive and inefficient form of transport, yet they were able to defeat the plague. They were truly a strange species.

The team perched atop a large machine designed to move the large cargo containers, giving them an overview of their target and the surrounding area. Metal boxes, probably used to store cargo, created a maze of the whole area, but there were still a few open spaces. Several sea-going vessels were docked in the distance, and one looked different that the others. It was smaller, and based on the weaponry, it was military. The Vicious One guessed that the vessel belonged to the Others.

'This is likely the end,' said the Vicious One. 'After our deaths, there will be none to summon the rest of the species. They too will likely die given time.'

'Then why do we fight?' asked the Pious One.

The Vicious One's mind sensed that it did not ask the question to be rebellious. It only wanted to know why it would fight to the death. But the Vicious One could not think of an answer that did not sound hollow in its mind. The planet was corrupted, the humans were corrupted, and bringing the species here would corrupt them, too. The Others defeated them.

The Vicious One showed its wounds to its team. Gangrenous flesh surrounded the opening, and it faintly smelled of death. 'The plague is real, and it will destroy us, no matter what the alchemists say about it. These corrupted humans are planning something. What it is, I do not know. But if there is any chance that their plans will help the Others to succeed, we must stop it. We cannot control what happens after our deaths, but before then, we will do what we can to make them fear us.'

The rest of the team stared silently. From birth, they were raised with the belief in the everlasting power of their species. Their minds knew, without any doubt, that the species's sojourn through the void would end, and they would find a new homeworld. Even with the slow decay of their culture and science and the steady loss of their population, they had refused to admit that the end would come in the form of death. But that was the truth that now faced them.

The Pious One spoke its secret name out loud. The shock running through the team was palpable. The Pious One had chosen death.

It spoke its secret name again, and this time the rest of the team repeated it, so that all could remember it. In turn, each of them spoke their secret name and the rest repeated it.

Finally, it was the Vicious One's turn to speak. The corruption soaked deeper into the body, and with every passing moment, its defenses grew weaker. 'I am unfit to speak my secret name.'

The Pious One growled. 'Your body is corrupted, and soon your mind will be, too. But your soul will always be yours. Do not let the others take that from you.'

The darkness the Others served needed souls. If the Vicious One spoke its secret name, maybe it would deny the Others another victory? It said its name out loud.

The team separated so that they could speak to the gods in their own way, offering the secret names of their friends so that they could be found after death. Then they regrouped and readied their minds and bodies for battle.

In an open area below, the woman had set a guard of eighty or so armed men in a wide perimeter around the vehicles that held the infected and the skulls of the Others. The men were normal, but the weapons they carried looked much bigger and more powerful than what the Vicious One faced before its capture in the prison. They set up a choke point, blocking access to the various sea-going vessels.

But that did not matter. The Vicious One leapt and came crashing down on two of the humans. Their bodies flattened under the Vicious One's weight, and their fluids sprayed out across the ground like a biological supernova. The Vicious One moved to its next targets, breaking their bodies and scattering the pieces, while the rest of the team fell from the sky and destroyed the humans.

Upon seeing the attack, the woman shouted a command, and her minions opened the containers on their vehicles and released a flood of infected humans. They rushed out, snarling and hungry, goaded on by the scent of fresh blood. There were far too many to even guess at their numbers. The woman yelled at them, sending them in the direction of the Vicious One and its team.

The fear from the other team members wafted through the air and mixed with the stench of the infected. It was the first time they had seen the infected, and the first sign that they would truly die soon. But the Vicious One could not share that fear with its comrades. It was already infected. It was already dead. What more could they do to it?

The Vicious One grabbed a human by its leg and flung it, still screaming, into the onrushing horde of infected. Several went down, and more jumped upon the human and started to feast upon it. Then the Vicious One charged head first into the mass of rotting bodies.

Skin split and bones crunched against the Vicious One's hard shell, and the infected became slop underfoot. It rammed its way into the battle until the infected surrounded it on all sides. The Vicious One thrashed its arms and stomped its feet. It had no plan, no targets. It let chaos guide its movements, let the anger in its body and mind drive it to kill more. A red haze filled the air, and infected blood covered the Vicious One's body, stinging its eyes and flowing into its mouth. But as soon as one went down, another took its place.

Infected teeth bit into its skin, but the Vicious One merely swatted the attacker away. Then another locked its jaws onto it, then another. The infected crawled atop each other, trying to find a spot of unbitten flesh, and their combined weight became too much for even the Vicious One's strength. The infected pulled it to the ground so that it could not move its limbs, and, bite by bite, they started tearing it apart.

A heavy mass slammed into the Vicious One, and the infected were knocked loose from its body. It rose to its feet, yanking off the remaining infected and dashing their bodies into the ground.

Next to the Vicious One, the Pious One scooped up two infected and mashed them together so that their flesh and blood became one. The rest of the team were in the thick of it, slashing and clawing, warriors all, if not by birth then by action.

The woman stood at the edge of the fray, observing the carnage. The Vicious One plowed through infected to get to her, and the woman stood her ground. Expecting some kind of trick, the Vicious One stopped before he reached the woman and waited for her to make the first move.

The expression on her face changed, but the Vicious One could not guess what emotion she felt. Then, coming from both sides, the Vicious One sensed the corruption. A group of cloaked humans formed a circle around the Vicious One. They removed their cloaks, and the Vicious One could feel the heat of excitement radiating from their veiny faces. Their claws and fangs, sharp and fiery, glistened in the moonlight.

In its condition, the Vicious One knew that it would fail in battle against the corrupted. Each of its injuries pulsed with the pain of infection, but the mind would not allow the body to fight it off. The energy needed to do so would put too much strain on the system. The Vicious One did the only thing it could.

The body and mind became one. The Vicious One felt a new clarity, as if it saw the universe from a new perspective, maybe even the perspective of a god. Strength flowed into its limbs, injuries and infections forgotten. It could feel its body working down to the cellular level, and it could track the individual electrochemical impulses through its mind. It felt more power than it could have imagined, but it would only last so long before the darkness within it merged with the soul.

The first corrupted bounded towards the Vicious One. It caught the human mid-air and slammed it into the ground, its head exploding and its guts spewing out of the opening. Two more charged in, the first falling under the Vicious One's claws, and the second getting turned into an improvised flail. The Vicious One used its weapon until the bones were pulverized and the corrupted was no more than a loose bag of flesh. But it served its purpose, and several more corrupted were dead or dying.

The final two corrupted squared off against the Vicious One, and rushed it at the same time. The Vicious One snatched one in its mouth and chomped down hard. The corrupted's foul, noxious flesh filled the Vicious One's mouth, and the excess spilled out the sides.

The other corrupted used its partner's death as an opportunity to leap onto the Vicious One's head. It stabbed its claws into the Vicious One's eye socket and wrapped its fingers around the eyeball. It tugged at and in one motion pulled the eye out and broke the optic nerve with an audible snap.

The Vicious One roared with a pain that even the merging of its mind and body could not hide. It grabbed the corrupted and held its torso between its hands. The corrupted slashed at it, digging through the skin, but the Vicious One ignored its attacks. It slowly squeezed the corrupted, applying a steady pressure until the viscera poured slowly from the corrupted's mouth like an amorphous animal slithering out of its burrow.

Behind it, the Vicious One heard the continued battle between its comrades and the infected. The woman was nowhere to be found, but the Vicious One had encountered her enough times to know the scent of her corruption.

'You are too late,' said a voice. No, it was many voices speaking as one. The voices mumbled in languages the Vicious One could not recognize, and it followed their sound to find the skulls of the others.

'You are too late,' they repeated. They spoke into its head, but the Vicious One heard them as though they had physical voices. They repeated the phrase over and over.

Something roared in the distance, and the Vicious One turned around to see a missile shoot into the air. Several more followed it. The Vicious One could sense the corruption contained within the missiles as they faded into the distant sky. They were spreading the infection around the planet. The Vicious One imagined that each one would explode over a major population center and rain the plague down on the humans. But if they eliminated the humans, how did they plan on corrupting the species?

The skulls kept chattering. The Vicious One turned its attention to them and destroyed them one by one. While it worked, it did not notice one final missile shoot up into the sky until it came back down mere moments later.

# CHAPTER TWENTY-TWO

In one moment, there was only the blackness of night above and the twinkling of electric lights in the city below. In the next, there was a storm of fire engulfing the sky and creating an infernal rain over Long Beach.

The explosion was small, only taking out one or two buildings, but Halley still braced himself as he watched the shock wave shoot out from the center of the blast. It shattered windows and uprooted trees and sent a cloud of smoke and dust into the air. When it reached Halley, it felt like a punch in the heart and a gunshot in the ear, but it did no real damage. And despite the morphine and tightly wrapped bandages, it still sent burning stings through his stump.

"What the hell is that woman doing?" said Wilcox. He glared at the lingering flames, and Halley could swear that he heard Wilcox growling like a hungry dog.

Rex floored it, and their truck blasted down the highway. The other vehicles behind them matched their speed. "She's not infecting the city, is she?"

Wilcox shook his head angrily. "That's exactly what she's doing. But why? There won't be anything left if the war starts again."

Halley looked back at the other vehicles and saw Jacey sitting in one of them, still tied up. Davis must be more important to Wilcox than Halley imagined if he decided to keep the girl. He turned back around. "Sir, if you don't mind me asking, what is happening?"

Wilcox glanced back at Halley. Halley expected the veins to pop up on his face again, but Wilcox seemed all right. "How much further to the port?" he asked Rex.

"Maybe another five or six miles," said the mercenary.

Wilcox adjusted himself to better face Halley. "You've always been loyal, and I'm sorry that I had to leave you out of all of this. But I needed to maintain legitimacy in the military. If you knew anything, it could have risked everything."

Halley studied the fire outside. "What do you mean by legitimate? I did all your dirty work."

"Yes. And even though everything was top secret, it was all official. If anybody found out about it, they wouldn't find anything suspicious. No one wants to talk about it, but this isn't the same world as it was before the war. The things I had you do are necessary for maintaining order."

"But I wasn't maintaining order, was I?"

"No. You were keeping my dealings with another group secret."

Halley eyeballed Rex. "What is this other group?"

"Not these mercenaries. They work for me. The other group . . . well, they're the real heroes of the war."

"What did they do?"

"They ended it. Cheung got all the credit, but he didn't invent anything. This group gave the weapon to me and Cheung. He invented the delivery system but got all the credit.

"And they didn't care. They didn't want to see the world die at the hands of the zombies. They wanted humans to live.

"What do they want now?"

Wilcox grit his teeth and snarled. "I thought they wanted power. Power for all of us. They're a large organization. All over the world. But not so big that they couldn't be crushed at any time. That's why they needed my help in the first place. I joined with them in exchange for a share of the prize at the end. I was going to bring you in on it, too."

Halley wasn't sure if he should have felt flattered.

"This organization was the first to realize that the zombie toxin was alien," Wilcox continued. "Even Cheung couldn't figure that out. But we knew that the war was just a way to soften us up before the real invasion. We've been preparing for the invasion ever since. And we figured that there might be some alien technology somewhere on this planet." He pointed at the large stone pillar in the back of the truck. "It could be used for creating new weapons. We would have a way to defeat the aliens, and we'd be steps ahead of every other world power trying to figure out the alien technology. It would have been a perfect opportunity to sweep in and claim the world as our own."

Incredible. Halley wanted to laugh. In the end, Wilcox was just a super-villain from a movie. "What about Davis. What's so special about him?"

Wilcox let out a hearty chuckle. "Nothing. There are hundreds, maybe thousands of people just like him. Those two things I killed, for example. But they wanted them, and they had me going all around the world to collect them. When I found out what they could do, I decided I needed one of my own."

"So you had me kidnap him without these people knowing."

"Cheung found a way to modify Davis's DNA and recombine it with another person's, make it better even, but I still need Davis until the transformation is complete."

"Why do you want Davis's powers?"

Wilcox stared out the window. Parts of the city burned, and the blue and red of emergency lights flashed through the streets. "Just in case they ever betray me."

Halley wondered how much more there was that he didn't know, and he wanted to ask for more, but there was a strange glow in Wilcox's eyes and a slight hint of dilating veins under his skin. Wilcox always knew that the organization would betray him. Or that he would betray them. They were the two forces in the world that could maybe defeat the aliens, and neither wanted the other to exist. Was Wilcox's side the right side?

The convoy pulled off the highway and followed the streets towards the port. Wilcox got on the radio to give his orders. "All right everyone, listen up. I don't want any prisoners. I can't risk any prisoners. These people aren't human, not anymore, so don't hesitate to keep killing them after they're dead. There's only one exception. A woman named Elise. She's not like the others. You'll know her when you see her."

Wilcox turned back around and handed a pistol to Halley. He looked at the arm stub. "Just stay back. There's not much fighting you can do."

Rex drove through the security gate and slowed the vehicle down. The convoy drove deeper into the port, down a narrow corridor of shipping containers, until they emerged in a wide open space. "Sir, I don't think there's much fighting for anyone to do."

"What the hell do you mean?" Wilcox asked, but the answer was apparent.

They drove over a battlefield, or what was once a battlefield. Bodies lay scattered about, most of them broken and spread out across the ground, and Halley could tell from the rotten stench that leaked into the truck that many of the bodies were zombies. Some still twitched or jolted as if waking from a dream, but Halley couldn't tell if it was because they were alive or if it was some leftover nerve impulses.

"What happened here?" Rex asked.

"It's a zombie army," Wilcox mused. "What is there plan?"

Rex stopped the truck and surveyed the surroundings. His eyes stopped in one direction. "Holy shit!" he screamed and jumped out.

Halley and Wilcox turned their heads. An alien barreled towards them, running on all fours and dripping gore from its fangs. Wilcox leapt out, and Halley tried to open the door, but remembered he didn't have a hand. He stuffed his gun into his pants and shoved the door open moments before the alien rammed head first into the truck and sent it tumbling through the air.

The stone pillar fell out of the truck and landed with a tiny shock wave. The alien glanced at the pillar and then at Wilcox. It was almost as if it could tell that Wilcox was the leader of the group.

Wilcox stood up and tore off his shirt. Veins curled up and down his chest and back, like tentacled hands grabbing at him. He stalked towards the alien, and the alien responded by kicking Wilcox firmly in the chest. The general flew backwards just inches off the ground and then scraped into the rough pavement, tearing open his veins. He kept rolling, spraying blood in circles around him, and Halley wondered if he would ever stop.

The mercenaries opened fire on the alien. Some of them jumped out of their vehicles and shot at the thing with their rifles. When the bullets hit the soft parts of the alien, they were sucked into the skin, and it looked as if nothing struck the spot. The big guns mounted on the back of the vehicles, however, did take a toll.

Chunks of alien flesh went hurtling through the air, and the wounds healed slower than those from the smaller weapons. The alien tried to protect itself by turning its hardened back towards the gunfire, but the bullets still cracked its shell, and sharp pieces splintered off and sprinkled on the ground.

In what Halley figured had to be a pain-induced rage, the alien pounced on the nearest truck and tucked its arms around the bottom. It stood up and forced its arms overhead, flinging the truck into the air. The truck somersaulted and landed upside-down on top of another truck. Under the crunching impact, the gunners from both trucks squirted out the sides like too much ketchup on a hamburger. The alien faced the other mercenaries.

Halley pulled his gun and started shooting, even though he knew it wouldn't do anything. Within seconds, he was empty, and even if he had an extra magazine, he didn't think he could reload one-handed.

Out of the corner of his eye, he saw Jacey jump out of her vehicle and run for cover, her hands still bound. Halley went after her, and together they hid behind a shipping container. With his one hand, Halley loosened the rope around her hands, and she shook herself free.

A scream stabbed through the air, and Rex flew overhead and plopped dead on the ground. The body was so twisted that Halley couldn't tell what part connected where.

"I don't think it's safe here," said Jacey.

Halley nodded. "I agree."

They ran off away from the alien and the battle, towards the exit. They passed back through the corridor of shipping containers until the front gate was in sight. But something blocked their path.

Jacey pointed. "Is that what I think it is?"

Whatever it was that exploded over the city worked fast. Dozens, maybe hundreds, of zombies headed in their direction, and they were only a few hundred yards away. Were they here by chance? Or were they summoned somehow? Halley didn't want to waste time thinking about it. He grabbed Jacey and pulled her away. This is all madness, he thought as they ran back down the way they just came.

"Let's find Wilcox," he said. "There's no way we can fight those things."

From the direction of the fight, the gunfire was much more sparse, and the death screams of the mercenaries was more frequent. Out of sight of the battle, Wilcox lay face down in a puddle of his own flesh. Halley hesitated to step onto the mess, but he grabbed the general's shoulder and heaved him onto his back. Road rash had taken away half his face, and that half was just a fleshy skull with an unblinking eyeball in its socket.

Wilcox could have been dead, but he inhaled sharply and sat up. The human side of his face didn't betray any pain.

Halley squatted down in front of Wilcox, trying to only make eye contact with the good side of his face. "Sir, there's an army of zombies headed this way. And the alien is killing off the rest of your men. There's no escape, and your the only one strong enough to fight."

Wilcox forced himself to his feet. "They're going to kill the world. Why?" He spoke mostly to himself, ignoring the difficulty he had forming the words with only half his lips. Saliva streamed out from his mouth and dangled like a vine.

He trudged past Halley and Jacey into a clearing that gave him a line of sight towards the zombies. They were closer now, and their growls told Halley that they could smell blood. When they caught sight of the general, they broke into a run.

Wilcox raised his arms to his side and started to laugh maniacally.

# CHAPTER TWENTY-THREE

There was a sense of unease in the air in the city of Long Beach. Fiona would expect it, especially after the explosion in the sky, but there was something more to it. The few people walking around appeared to be in a daze, almost as if they were unaware of what just happened.

Davis slammed on the brakes and barely avoided plowing through a crowd of people running across the street. They all followed each other, fear in their eyes and panic in their screams.

"Is there another fire?" Fiona asked. "Is Wilcox trying to burn this city, too?" She held the crystal closer to her body, as if she thought that someone would try to steal it.

Davis rolled down his window and stuck his head outside. A faint scent of smoke came into the truck.

About five minutes had passed since the explosion over the city. As she watched the fireball expand over the city, Fiona thought it was a nuclear explosion. She thought Dr. Cheung had somehow managed to spread his disease all the way to Long Beach. A few months into the war, the nuclear option was tested over a few of the smaller cities in the world, and seeing the explosion in the sky made Fiona think that the war really was starting again.

The crowd of people passed, and Davis started rolling the truck down the street. The car screeched as he stopped for another group of people running by. Most kept running, but a few stopped and stared at Fiona and Davis. Their dead eyes were the only thing Fiona needed to see.

"Go! Run them over!" she yelled.

Davis didn't have to be told twice. He floored it and crunched the zombies under his wheels.

"All those people running . . . " Fiona started.

"Their running from hordes of zombies," said Davis. "How can they turn so fast?"

Fiona nodded. "They were still fresh. Almost alive. I saw it." She thought about how fast Ramecker changed after Cheung killed her.

Even while he navigated the streets, Davis's eyes seemed to look back in time. "These aren't the same things we saw back in the war. It's a new kind of zombie. It transforms people faster."

Fiona glanced behind her. Five canisters rattled in the back seat, each full of Cheung's weapon. Not even a bullet to the head could kill a zombie as well as the weapon. "How much area does one of those canisters cover?" she asked.

Davis stared at her, wide-eyed and ignoring the road. "What are you thinking?"

"We can't let the zombies overrun the city. We have to stop them before they get too far."

The muscles in Davis's jaw knotted and unknotted while his fingers tried to squeeze the life out of the steering wheel. Fiona knew he wanted to go after Elise, and after years in his cell, he had his chance.

"You'll never find your answers if there's another war," Fiona said.

Davis's face relaxed. "Cheung told me that each canister can cover over a hundred square miles. But we'd have to release the gas from someplace high." He surveyed the surroundings and pointed at a tower. "That should be good."

Fiona followed Davis's finger and felt her guts melt. It was a taller building than any around it, but it was closer to where the explosion took place, and the people they saw running were all headed in the opposite direction. Before she could voice her concerns, Davis wheeled the car around and headed towards the tower.

They didn't see anyone or anything on the drive over, but the bloody patches on the ground gave evidence that something bad happened. The glass on every building had been blown out by the force of the explosion, and as they approached the tower, the air took on a strange orange glow. It could have been from the fire, but to Fiona it seemed as if there was something unnatural about the glow. Kind of the way the alien pillar emitted an unnatural light.

Davis pulled up in front of the tower and killed the engine. "I don't see anything. I think we're safe."

They both got out, and Davis grabbed one of his many rifles and tossed it to Fiona. To catch the flying gun, she had to drop the alien crystal.

"Just leave that thing," Davis said, pointing at the crystal. He slung a rifle around his back and took a pistol in one hand and one of the canisters of Cheung's weapon in the other.

"What if it gets stolen?"

"It's a rock. I don't think zombies are smart enough to care. It's safe."

"What if a human steals it?"

Davis started towards the entrance. "They're too busy getting eaten to care."

Davis turned his back, and Fiona tossed the crystal into the truck and slammed the door. It didn't feel right leaving the crystal by itself. It was more important than she could imagine, and she knew it.

It had been years since she held a rifle, and now twice in one day she had to use one. She had to admit that it felt normal in her hands. The weight was comfortable, even.

Davis cleared out some shards of glass left over in the door frame, and he stepped through the opening. Fiona followed, listening for any growls, trying to feel hidden eyes on her. Strange shadows, created by the orange glow, danced across the interior and provided a hiding place for the undead. "Do you think there are any in here?" she asked.

"Don't know. If they saw the big fire earlier, maybe they panicked and left. Or they just went home for the evening." He tried the elevator door, but the button didn't respond. "I don't think it's working."

Fiona looked around. "The stairs are over there."

Davis nodded. "You go first."

"What?"

"You've got a bigger gun."

"Can't you just tell the zombies to go screw themselves?"

Davis hesitated. "I'm not so sure that'll work that well. Like I said, these are different than the ones back in the war."

With the orange glow from outside, the door leading to the stairwell looked like the gates of hell. "Okay, I'll go first." With one hand, Fiona grabbed the door knob, and with the other she held up her rifle. The door opened to emptiness, and both Fiona and Davis let out a sigh of relief.

Each step echoed hollowly, and even with the lights, the top of the stairwell disappeared into darkness, even though the building wasn't more than ten stories tall. It was like looking down into a bottomless pit, and Fiona feared that if she jumped she would lose her connection with gravity and fall up into the abyss.

From above, a doorway slammed open and startled Fiona. She grabbed the handrail to prevent herself from jumping off into space. Footsteps crashed down the stairwell and got closer and closer. Fiona raised her rifle and prepared herself.

At the next corner, a man slammed into the wall, smearing his blood across the white paint. He tumbled down the next steps and landed like a rag doll in front of Fiona. She pointed her rifle at him, but didn't pull the trigger. The skin around his jaw was peeled down and hung around his neck like a kerchief. The sounds coming out of his mouth could have been growls or they could have been his ruined voice.

But his eyes convinced Fiona not to shoot. They were terrified, sad, pained. Alive. Fiona knew what she had to do, but she couldn't.

Davis lunged forward and grabbed the man by the collar. He yanked him to his feet and dragged him over to the handrail. With a simple shove, he sent the man over the edge. The handrail rang out like a bell as the man hit it once and then a second time. He hit the ground with a splat like rotten fruit.

Fiona looked over the edge. It was only darkness, like above. "Why did you do that?"

"You know why." Davis stepped around her and continued the climb up the stairs.

Fiona did know why, but she did not want to accept it. The old ways of the war were coming back.

The darkness below would not clear out, no matter how hard Fiona wished it would. "What if he was like you? What if he was able to survive?"

The sound of Davis's footsteps stopped. The silence between the two hurt Fiona's ears. At last, Davis spoke. "Something up there attacked him. We better be careful it doesn't get us, too."

They followed the trail of the man's blood, finding the door he came through. Davis put his ear to the door and tried to listen to anything on the other side. He shook his head.

The darkness above started to dissipate, and Fiona could see the ladder and trapdoor that led to the roof. They hurried up, and Fiona was the first to climb the ladder. She gave the door a push, and nothing happened.

She looked around. "Damn. It's a padlock."

Davis twisted his neck to look up at the lock tucked away in the shadows at the corner of the door. "All right. Get down." He raised his rifle and took aim. "I hope no one hears this."

Fiona quickly ducked out of the way and covered her ears. "Yeah, me, too. Does that actually work?"

Davis gave her a blank stare and a shrug. Then he took a shot. The gunshot boomed all the way down the stairwell and back up. Covering her ears did nothing; Fiona still heard the ringing in her head.

Davis said something.

"What?" asked Fiona.

"I missed," Davis repeated. The bullet burrowed a little hole right next to the padlock.

The ringing still took up most of her hearing, but Fiona thought that a faint growling came from below them. "Listen," she said, looking over the edge. The darkness seemed to be slowly creeping up from the bottom.

"I don't hear anything," said Davis. "Fire in the hole."

Fiona barely had time to cover her ears. Davis smiled after the shot, and took a second one right away.

The broken bits of the padlock clattered down and bounced down the stairs. Davis said something that Fiona couldn't hear, and he pushed her towards the ladder.

She started to climb when she heard it. The zombies coming up the stairwell were unmistakable now. "They're coming," she told Davis.

He cupped his hand to his ear. "What?"

She pointed down. There was nothing to see, but she hoped the message was clear.

Davis nodded and urged her to head to the roof. She pushed open the trapdoor, and the orange glow flooded the stairwell. She climbed up and stepped out onto the gravel. Davis passed the canister to her, and the howls of the zombies came so loud even Davis heard them.

"Get that thing started," he said and dropped back into the stairwell. The sound of gunshots burst from the trapdoor.

Fiona dragged the canister to the middle of the roof and set it upright. She hoped it worked the way Davis told her it would. She pulled the pin and twisted the knob to open the canister.

With a hiss, a thin stream of green smoke rose into the air. Fiona backed away, even if she knew it was harmless to humans. She watched the geyser of smoke rise higher and higher to where it would saturate the atmosphere and eventually come back down. Then it would kill the zombies. Fiona let herself smile. She ended the war before it even started. She knew she could move on now.

Fiona's heart almost broke through her ribs as Davis nearly flew out of the trapdoor. He ran towards her, reloading as he moved. "There's a lot more of them than I thought. I think this is an apartment building."

A zombie poked its head out of the trapdoor, and Fiona took a few shots to send it back down. Then another came up, faster than Fiona or Davis could shoot. And another followed.

The zombies were fresh, free of the decay that would affect them in time. Their muscles moved with precision and without the restraints of a conscious mind. As soon as Davis or Fiona took one out, another crawled up.

It would only be moments before there were too many to fight, and Fiona was almost out of ammo. She slung her rifle on her back and grabbed the canister. She tilted the opening so that the green smoke shrouded the zombies in fog. At the end of the war, seeing the zombies melt when they came into contact with the smoke was one of Fiona's favorite memories. This moment wasn't so bad.

Davis lowered his weapon, and Fiona set up the canister again. The hissing from the canister had not gotten any weaker. There was still plenty left. Fiona smiled, and to her surprise, Davis smiled back.

Then his face went blank and his eyes became cold. He raised his rifle with one hand and took a shot. Inches from her face, Fiona could feel the heat escaping from the muzzle. Davis grabbed her and shoved her behind him. He kept shooting until he was empty.

Zombies, dozens of them, slipped from behind the green fog. The weapon had no effect. Their eyes were as hungry as they had ever been, and their teeth clicked as they anticipated their next meal.

Davis flipped his gun around and clubbed a zombie's head open. He shoved one back into the fog, and he followed it in, disappearing.

Fiona grabbed her rifle. She was alone.

# Chapter Twenty-Four

The Vicious One whipped a corrupted human into the ground and tossed the remains away. Another tried to crawl away, leaving a trail of organs from its missing bottom half. The Vicious One took a handful of the guts and reeled the corrupted in and finished it off with a foot to the head.

There couldn't possibly be anymore of the corrupted or the infected, the Vicious One thought. After destroying the skulls of the Others, another wave of the corrupted attacked, and the effort required to kill them bordered on excessive. The plague flowing through its veins caused actual, physical pain. It was as if the Vicious One was being shredded into finer and finer pieces from the inside out. Keeping the mind and the body merged proved to be an impossible task. It required too much energy, and the Vicious One needed that energy in case there was a bigger enemy ahead. And merging the mind and the body let the darkness get too close.

The woman got away, but the Vicious One sensed that she was not too far, though its mind did not work at full capacity. She had a plan, and she would want to see it to fruition before making her escape.

In the distance, the orange glow left by the explosion turned night into unnatural day. The humans there would most assuredly be infected by now. The Vicious One did not feel any pity for the humans, but it could not understand how the woman could purposefully infect so much of her own kind. And she sent it around the planet. In time, the plague would ensure the complete destruction of the humans. If any of the Others remained, what physical beings would serve as their surrogates? How would the destruction of this planet aid the spread of their darkness around the galaxy?

A strange shift in the air currents and the gravitational field stirred the Vicious One's mind. The rest of its team approached. Though each was covered in gore, and the Pious One seemed to be healing from multiple fractures in its carapace, the Vicious One sensed that none were severely hurt or, more importantly, infected.

But that did not concern it. The Pious One held the gravity drive in its hands. It set the pillar down in front of the Vicious One. 'A new group of humans were in possession of this,' said the Pious One.

The written instructions on the outside of the gravity drive used archaic vocabulary, but the Vicious One still knew how to use it. The device was so rare it had never seen one, but every member of the species was instructed in its use. It was the only way to move something as massive as the species's fleet through space without the energy demands of creating a wormhole or the effects of faster than light travel.

'It must be destroyed,' said the Vicious One.

The rest of the team could not hide their agitation with the Vicious One's suggestion. 'But the plague has been re-released on the humans,' said the Pious One. 'When they are dead, the species can harvest this planet.'

'So we . . . you hide and wait for the destruction of humanity?' asked the Vicious One.

The rest gave their agreement.

'But how long can we hide? The humans have defeated this plague before. Do you not expect them to do it again?'

The Pious One started to speak but decided no to.

'And one more concern,' said the Vicious One. 'The Others and their corrupted humans will continue their search for the gravity drive. We are not of this planet.

Where can you hide where you cannot be found? The Others will track you down and send the corrupted after you until you are all infected or dead. Whether it be this day or one in the future, the Others will have the gravity drive before the infection kills the humans. And that would mean the death of our species.'

The infection sent a wave of pain through the Vicious One's body. It did what it could to block out the pain, but the reach the plague had in the Vicious One's body was too great. Its knees wobbled, and it slumped forward. It caught the gravity drive and used it to stand back up. The team's concern wafted off of them, but none made any move to help. It would have been rude.

The Vicious One held onto the gravity drive and examined it. 'There is no power in this object.'

'It is as I found it,' said the Pious One. 'I did not sense any power source nearby.'

Then the gravity drive was useless. The Others, at least for now, would be unable to bring the rest of the species to this planet.

In the Vicious One's ever-weakening mind, it thought it felt an approaching corruption. The change in demeanor of the rest confirmed that something was happening.

'The infected,' said the Pious One. 'The ones created by the explosion. They are here.'

'How many are there?' asked the Vicious One.

'Too many. Far more than we could possibly handle.'

Were they drawn to the gravity drive? Did the woman summon them? The Vicious One dismissed those ideas. Humans did not possess the anatomy to communicate that way. The only ones to be able to do so were the Others. But their skulls lay shattered on the ground.

'There is something here,' said the Vicious One. 'One of the Others.'

'We would sense it if it existed,' said the Pious One. 'You have killed them all.'

'No,' replied the Vicious One. 'It is here. It is drawing the infected here. It knows we have the gravity drive.'

'Then we destroy it now.' The Pious One snatched the gravity drive out of the Vicious One's hands and hammered it into the ground. Dust and dirt and chips of stone flew into the air, but the gravity drive sustained no damage.

'It will take more than violence to destroy it,' said the Vicious One. 'If we are to stop the Others from getting the gravity drive, we must kill the one controlling the infected.' It pointed at the Pious One. 'Come with me.'

The rest knew what they had to do without the Vicious One saying so. The merging of their minds and bodies released a wave of energy.

'My friends,' said the Vicious One. 'Our souls will be collected together soon enough.'

They turned and headed towards the nearing wave of corruption.

'What do we do with this?' asked the Pious One, motioning at the gravity drive.

'You will keep it safe. Do not let any infected or corrupted humans get it.'

With pain shooting out from each of its wounds, the Vicious One headed for the military vessel. The woman had to be there. The Pious One followed, holding tight to the gravity drive.

No humans, normal or otherwise, stood guard around the vessel. The Vicious One instructed the Pious One to stay outside and hide and to keep the gravity drive safe. Then it scaled the hull of the vessel and hopped onto the deck.

Now that it was on the vessel, the Vicious One could better sense the woman's presence. She was here, along with several other corrupted humans. It followed its sense to a large door in the deck that opened up into the interior.

It pulled the large metal doors open and peered inside. The woman was there with several more like her. They stood in a circle looking up at the Vicious One as if they were waiting for it. The orange glow from the sky provided the only light inside.

The Vicious One tried to merge its mind and body, but it had so little energy left and the infection was too intense to make the merging possible. It needed something more to make it happen. But that did not matter. It would kill them all anyway.

It jumped down into the center of the circle, and it took a muscle-tearing effort just to not collapse. None of the corrupted moved.

'I know you wish to fight,' said a voice. It went straight into the Vicious One's mind. Another scholar.

The chamber was dark, but the movement of the air currents against the Vicious One's skin suggested that it was also empty. Only the corrupted and their master were in it.

'Soon, you will be one of us,' said the voice.

The Vicious One tried to push it out of his mind, but it failed. 'Never,' it said, even as the infection sent another surge of pain through its body.

The humans broke apart their circle and stood in a line together. The Vicious One followed their eyes to the opposite end of the chamber.

Something emerged from the darkness and stood in the light with the Vicious One. It was double the size of the Vicious One, and though rot consumed its flesh, its muscles bulged with power, and its fangs and claws were still as sharp as fire. It was not a scholar, a weak body easily destroyed by the infection. It was a warrior. A monster created and bred to endure pain and torment with joy.

The warrior spoke with its physical voice. 'Even now, I am bringing together the parts of the gravity drive. We will summon the species here and give them the gift of darkness.'

The Vicious One could not let that happen. It could not let the species fall to such a fate.

Fueled by anger, fueled by the darkness, its body and mind started to merge. It became one with itself, but the darkness grabbed a hold of its soul, and The Vicious One knew that the darkness would never let go.

# CHAPTER TWENTY-FIVE

Green smoke swirled as a zombie charged, its claws raised for the kill. His weapon long gone, Davis swung his fist at the zombie. His knuckles connected with the zombie's jaw, and teeth cracked as they were forced together. Davis took another swing, and the zombie's head spun until it faced backwards.

The sudden increase in strength surprised Davis, but he remained focused and used the strength to his advantage. His fingers gripped hard enough to tear windpipes from throats. His strength increased to yank arms from shoulders. His legs moved fast enough to lead him from one kill to the next. As one zombie after another died at his hands, he could feel himself moving closer to letting his bloodlust take control.

And he wanted it. Losing himself to violence would grant him a level of strength he couldn't imagine. It would be the next step in forgetting the Michael Davis of the forgotten past. But something kept him from giving in.

Outside of the fog, he could hear Dr. Todd shooting at the zombies that escaped his grasp. He stormed out of the smoke and found a few zombies on the ground with bullet holes in their faces. Even more surrounded Dr. Todd.

She stood on the ledge, firing at any zombie that got close. She would keep firing until the zombies were finished or she ran out of ammo. And if she did run out of ammo, the drop from the ledge was a better option than getting turned into dinner.

Davis didn't want it to get to that point. "Hey!" he shouted. The zombies stopped and looked at him. "All of you, jump off."

Without hesitation, they crept up to the edge of the building, ignoring Dr. Todd, and threw themselves over. The doctor watched them fall, and she cringed as each of them went splat at the bottom. Davis was in shock. Never had he such control over the zombies. Even in the lab.

Whether from the excitement of battle or from seeing so many bodies plunge off the side of a building, Dr. Todd started to look ill, and Davis had to pull her back off the ledge before she took a dive herself.

Her balance was off, and she fell into Davis. A second later, she screamed and pushed him away. As she fell backwards, she started shooting at him.

Davis didn't know what gave him more of a shock, getting shot at or dodging every bullet. He weaved his way through the rain of lead until he grasped the barrel of Dr. Todd's rifle and yanked it out of her hands.

"It's me," he said.

She stared at him, fearful, disbelieving.

Davis didn't know what could be the problem. He wondered if he was covered in zombie guts, and he looked down at his hands.

It was blood on his arms, but it didn't belong to any zombie. He tried to wipe it off, but it belonged to him, and it pulsed through veins thick enough to pop to the surface of his skin. He followed the thick red veins up his arms to his throat and onto his face.

His hands shook with panic. Whatever caused the increase in strength had to have caused this transformation to his body. He dropped to his knees and drooped his head. Am I even human anymore? he asked himself.

Dr. Todd calmed down and stood next to Davis. The hissing from the canister ended as the last of the useless weapon escaped into the sky. The only zombie sounds came from the death rattles of the ones Davis didn't pulp into oblivion.

"It's over now," said Dr. Todd.

"What?"

"Your face, it's back to normal."

Davis touched his cheeks and jaw and forehead, feeling for the raised bumps of veins under his skin. They were gone, as were the veins on his arms. But Davis knew that whatever normalness Dr. Todd saw was a lie. It was just a mask that covered up the freak, the zombie, inside him. One day it would take over and never let go.

"I guess the war is starting over again," he said. He got up and kicked the canister over.

"It's not a total bust," said Dr. Todd. "I can make a new weapon." She rushed her words like a little kid bragging about a false achievement.

"How? Once the zombies spread, you won't have a lab or equipment."

"Don't worry about that. This is not the same world as the last time. We're different. We're prepared. The last time, everyone was confused and scared. Now, we'll fight back. I know it." Her voice grew more confident as she spoke.

Davis listened to her, and thought on her words. The war, or at least what he could remember of it, was about survival. It was day in and day out of killing. Sometimes it was zombies that needed killing, sometimes it was people like Wolff. The violence was petty and cruel and only served to get a person to the next morning.

But that was the old world. An old world built up over thousands of years of history and traditions. A world built up by generations of people long dead. But today's world was different. It was new, it was what the survivors could make of it. It was theirs.

In this new world, people wouldn't be fighting just for survival. They would be fighting for something they created, something that would outlast them and pave the way towards the future.

Stuck in his cell, Davis never did anything to get him out of the old war. His mind was stuck in the mentality of that war and not the new world. It was his last prison.

"What do you need?" he asked Dr. Todd.

"The canisters, at least. They're useless right now anyway. And I'll need samples of the zombies' DNA. I guess with a new war I should be able to get that easily."

Davis ripped a zombie's arm out of its socket. The meat squelched as Davis worked it free. "Just in case, you're taking a sample with you." He held the arm out to Dr. Todd.

"You can hold onto it for now," she said as she raised her hands protectively. "Let's get back to the truck."

Davis led the way back down the stairwell. There were no more zombies, which worried Davis more than if there were a few stragglers. He expected a few of them to not make it to the roof, but this seemed like they made a conscious decision to leave.

In the lobby, Davis wrapped the zombie arm in a plastic trash bag. Outside, the orange glow still dominated the night sky, though it started to fade. He tossed the arm in the bed of the truck, and Dr. Todd went to the passenger side door, which looked ajar from Davis's point of view.

"No, no, no, no," she said and swung open the door. She poked her head into the truck and swung it around as she looked around the seats.

"What is it?" asked Davis.

"The crystal is gone," she murmured.

Davis opened his door and started searching through the car. Then he checked underneath and around. It shouldn't have been hard to find as it was a big rock. But just as Dr. Todd said, it was gone.

"Who could have taken it?" she wondered out loud.

"It was the zombies." Davis said it with a definiteness that he could not explain.

"You said that they wouldn't do that."

"They wouldn't. It was something else." When they were arriving, all the zombies in the streets were headed in the same direction, as if compelled to by some kind of force. "I have to go after them."

Dr. Todd stood next to Davis. "No, we have to go after them."

Davis pressed the car keys into her hand. "It's going to take a few weeks for everyone to get organized once this war really starts going. You've already got a head start. You need to do your research on the new weapon."

Her fingers closed around the keys, but she remained silent.

"There's some more guns in the back of the truck," said Davis. "No one's around, so you're probably safe if you raid a grocery store. And a gas station."

Dr. Todd started to speak. Davis shook his head.

"Just get going. That weapon is the best chance of ending this war fast."

A protest started to form on her lips, but she gave up. "I'll get it done," she said. She hopped in the car and started up the engine. "Do you need a ride?"

Davis had no idea how far he had to go. "No, I'll be okay."

"Hey, good luck. After the war, we'll find something for you."

Davis tried to smile but could not do it. "Good luck to you, too."

Dr. Todd drove slowly away, and picked up speed the farther away she got. Davis watched her disappear into the distance. He didn't think they would meet again.

Despite the orange glow and empty streets and the occasional body laying around, the city felt quite peaceful. It was a new world, and he wanted to see it thrive.

But that was something else he didn't think that he would see. But he could stop Wilcox or Elise or whatever else was out there from getting that crystal.

He broke into a run, letting the new strength, the darkness, inside him take over his weak human body.

# Chapter Twenty-Six

The onrush of zombies enveloped Wilcox. They swarmed over him as easily as if he were a pile of dust in their way.

Halley didn't feel sad watching him go. Even though he'd worked alongside the general for years, seeing the man die barely stirred any emotion in him. It just happened, but he still watched and waited for Wilcox to re-emerge.

Jacey sprinted for a few steps then came back and grabbed Halley's good arm. "We can't just stand here," she said. The force she used to pull Halley's arm was enough to hurt the stump.

The zombies kept coming, and Wilcox was still drowned in their flood. Halley nodded. "Okay, okay," he murmured.

They ran without knowing their direction, without a plan on where to hide. The port covered a wide area, but the shipping containers trapped them like rats in a maze, and the thundering of the zombies' footsteps and the drone of their growling seemed to get louder with each passing moment.

Halley grabbed Jacey and almost had to battle her to get her to stop. "We can't keep running."

She tried to shake off his grasp. "They're getting closer."

"We have to get up somewhere high, where we can defend ourselves."

"Then let's climb one of these things," said Jacey, pointing at a shipping container. There were hundreds of the containers, all stacked neatly in rows.

"It's too tall, and I can't climb it with one arm."

Jacey looked around. "There."

She pointed about one hundred yards away at an eighteen-wheeler with a shipping container hitched to it. They'd be able to crawl up the front of the truck and stand on the container, a little island that they could defend. They headed towards it and picked up their pace as the snarling of zombies grew heavier on their ears.

Jacey gave Halley a boost onto the hood of the truck. Climbing with three limbs proved more difficult than Halley could have imagined, but he made it to the top. Jacey scrambled up with much more ease.

The rows of shipping containers blocked out the view of any zombies, but the ground vibrating as they moved assured Halley that they were there. Several ships were docked, and Halley wondered if their crews knew what was happening. If they did, they'd try to make for the ocean, probably the safest place during a zombie infestation.

There was also a naval vessel. A destroyer, Halley thought. Or a cruiser. Whatever it was, it had to be the source of the missiles. The source of the explosion over Long Beach. The group that Wilcox aligned himself with probably headquartered themselves there.

No matter how secret they were, they scared Wilcox enough that he injected himself with Davis's zombie-infected blood. What could be the driving force behind them? They weren't interested in power like Wilcox thought. That was the only thing Wilcox cared about, so he projected that desire onto others. But if this secret group wanted power, they wouldn't have released the zombie plague back onto the world. There would be no world left in the end.

Jacey said something. Halley ignored her to focus on his thoughts. The secret group knew something that Wilcox didn't. Something that gave them the confidence to carry out their plans. They knew they were going to win.

"Something's coming!" Jacey yelled. She grabbed Halley by the stump to get his attention. The pain dropped him to his knees, and then he heard what concerned Jacey. It was the screech and crash of metal, the ravenous yowls of zombies gorging on flesh, and the roars of unearthly creatures.

A tidal wave of zombies broke through the rows of shipping containers, toppling them and pushing them aside. Dozens, maybe hundreds, of them poured out, each slithering and clawing over one another. At the center of their attention were three aliens.

The zombies crawled onto the aliens like ants over a half-dead wasp. The aliens slashed and tore at them until red rained from the sky and blanketed the surrounding horde, but there were too many. The occasional glimpse Halley got of the aliens showed deep wounds, some going as deep as the bone. The aliens weren't fighting for their lives, those were surely over. But they fought with a ferocity born of their conviction.

The zombies kept surging, getting closer to Halley and Jacey. The aliens crushed more and more of the zombies but did nothing to slow their onslaught.

By the time Halley realized that the zombies would eventually get to the truck, Jacey was already scrambling down. Jacey fled, and Halley followed her, glancing back to see if any zombies chased them. They all seemed too preoccupied with the aliens.

"This way," said Halley, and he ran towards the naval vessel.

It was a massive ship, but as he and Jacey got closer, Halley could have sworn that he saw it move. He couldn't imagine the amount of force necessary to rock a ship like that, but the second time it moved convinced him that something was going on inside.

Several people ran down the gangplank just before another jolt sent the gangplank tumbling into the water. Jacey hesitated at the sight of them, but Halley urged her forward.

"They're going to kill us," she said.

"And so are the zombies," responded Halley.

While some of the people watched the ship, some watched Halley and Jacey approach. One in particular seemed the most interested. Halley recognized her as Elise, the woman in charge. She held up her hand to stop two of her flunkies when they rushed forward to intercept Halley and Jacey.

"It's Captain Halley, correct?" said Elise.

"Major. I know you are behind all of this destruction. And I know that you have a plan to survive it all. I want to join you."

Jacey couldn't express her shock. She started backing away, jaw slack and eyes wide. Halley seized her arm and glared at her until she submitted.

Elise looked more amused at Halley's offer than annoyed. The ship swayed side to side, and water sloshed up onto land. Her people watched, but Elise kept her eyes on Halley. "What can you give us that I don't have?"

"The military. I've worked with General Wilcox for years. I know all the secrets. I can get you access to whatever you need."

Elise laughed. "What makes you think I don't have all that already?"

Halley held back his response. "I can also get you Michael Davis. We stole him from you, and I can give him back."

"How?"

He pushed Jacey forward. "This girl. She knows Davis. Hold her hostage and Davis will come for her."

Jacey's fist drove into Halley's nose so fast and so hard there was no way he could have defended against it. Blood poured out of his nostrils like a waterfall, and Halley fell to one knee.

Halley ignored the pain. "I know Davis. He acts tough, but he cares about other people. You'll catch him."

Elise smiled at Halley's statement. It could have almost been a sneer. "I guess you don't know Davis as well as you thought. We don't need the girl. Or Davis."

Halley wondered if Elise was going to kill him and Jacey. The same thoughts probably passed through Jacey's mind as she kicked Halley in the stump.

The pain was so intense that he didn't feel anything at first. The world just started spinning, and a million Elises and Jaceys started revolving around his head. Then nausea exploded out of his gut and into his head and eyes, creating so much pressure Halley lost control of his muscles and collapsed. Finally, the pain sliced through his arm with the intensity of lightning and ice. Halley suddenly wished that Elise would have just killed him.

Through tearing eyes, Halley watched Jacey run.

"Let her go. We don't need her," said Elise. "But maybe we can find a use for the major."

The ship rocked again, and the force behind the movement was so great the ship nearly tipped over. After it righted itself, metal creaked and crunched, and an alien flew straight up out of the deck. It arced at the height of its flight and came crashing back down to earth. The sight was so unbelievable that Halley forgot his pain.

Bruises and lacerations covered the alien, and it should have let itself die, but it got to its feet and faced the ship. Though he knew nothing about aliens, Halley recognized the rage in the alien's roar.

Another alien crawled out of the ship and leapt onto land. The first alien, though beat up and broken, had a certain dangerous grace in its build. Not with the second one. It was a giant brute, and there was nothing to hide that fact.

The bigger alien charged towards the other. The smaller one tried to counter, but it ended up getting its throat caught in its enemy's powerful grasp. The monster raised its clawed hand to finish the fight.

From above, bounding over shipping containers, a third alien joined the battle. It carried the large stone pillar, and it brought the pillar down on the large alien's head as it landed. Chunks of skin blasted away from the alien's head, revealing a skull deformed by bulbous growths.

The alien batted away the nearest of Elise's people with the pillar while its companion worked its way free from the monster's grasp. Halley recognized the pillar as the one that Wilcox had in his truck. The large alien and Elise seemed to take notice, too.

Elise ordered her people to stay out of the fight, but they continued to watch. Halley knew this was his chance to escape. He struggled to his feet and made it a few steps before bumping into one of Elise's people.

The man put a veiny, clawed hand on Halley's shoulder and forced him to his knees. "You wanted to be a part of this, didn't you?" he said. "Watch. This is the moment when history changes."

Halley obeyed. It was what he did best.

# Chapter Twenty-Seven

The zombies led Davis right where he expected. What he didn't expect was the carnage surrounding him.

Innumerable zombie bodies littered the ground at the port. The blood was so thick it felt like walking through a marsh. Davis could only stare in amazement. Even a battalion of well-armed men would have had trouble causing this much damage to an incoming zombie horde. The only explanation was that something inhuman could have caused the damage. And it wasn't Elise. The zombies were her pets.

It had to be something not from this planet.

Some of the zombies still breathed air, their limbless bodies flopping around in the blood like a Frankenstein combination of fish and chicken nugget. Davis took care of them as quickly as possible. He didn't want them to cause him problems later, but he still had to catch up with the crystal before it got into Elise's hands.

One zombie took Davis by surprise. It rested on its haunches surrounded by mutilated bodies. It feasted on an arm, tearing at it with its teeth to separate tendons from bone and sucking and slurping up all the little bits of blood and fat. None of its injuries appeared particularly harmful to the undead, but somehow it avoided the mysterious call that all the other zombies answered.

Davis crept up behind it. A quick snap of the neck and a thorough stomping would finish it off for good. He got close, then the zombie whipped its meal into Davis's face. The heavy bones contacted Davis's chin and clicked his teeth together. He stumbled back and slipped in the grime, falling with a splash in a pile of limbs and organs.

The zombie standing over him was missing half its face, and though red stained the other half, Davis recognized Wilcox instantly. He chomped on a dangling piece of skin like it was a plug of chewing tobacco. Everything about him screamed zombie, but his eyes were still human. And then Davis noticed the thick veins curling up Wilcox's neck and onto his face.

Davis scrambled to his feet and faced Wilcox, every muscle in his body ready to fight. "Cheung used whatever's inside of me to turn you into this, didn't he?"

Wilcox spat out his bit of skin. "Have you felt the power within you? It's intoxicating." Little flecks of blood and saliva squirted out from the spaces in his teeth on the lipless side of his face.

"Turning into a zombie is not what anybody would want."

"Are you sure about that? I know your memory's bad."

Davis stepped forward and raised his fist. "What do you mean?"

Wilcox held up a hand to indicate that he wasn't in the fighting mood. "I think I have what you're looking for. I mean, everyone's looking for it, so you must be, too." He kicked aside some corpses until he revealed the crystal. It lay in a puddle of blood, but none of the blood clung to it. It was clean.

Wilcox picked it up. "I thought it a bit odd that a zombie would be carrying this thing, so I killed it and every other zombie that tried to pick it up. That wasn't easy."

"What is it?"

"It's power. It's technology so advanced our primitive minds couldn't understand it. It's what will allow me to shape the world in my image."

"You're not shaping anything. It's those other people, the ones unleashing the zombies, who are in control. They want that thing, and they probably know how to use it. We destroy it."

Wilcox cackled and stretched his jaw so wide his cheek split. "You have no vision. With this I will win the upcoming war."

Davis didn't feel like listening to any speeches. His fist crashed into Wilcox's exposed skull and teeth scattered like confetti. Wilcox dropped the crystal and instantly returned the attack.

Three blows sunk into Davis's gut, squeezing acid out of his gut and into his throat. Davis spewed the bitter liquid out of his mouth and into Wilcox's face, following up with a swift kick to the general's nuts.

Wilcox trapped Davis's leg between his thighs and wrenched him to the ground. Davis's face splashed into the zombie guts, and Wilcox's booted foot slammed into his skull and forced his face deeper in. The red liquid burned his nostrils as he inhaled, and the lack of air burned his lungs even more. He pushed against the ground, trying to raise himself up, but Wilcox's foot felt like it weighed a ton. Wilcox twisted his foot, giving Davis the choice to drown in zombie viscera or wait until his head exploded under the pressure.

Panic set in, and Davis's strength started to rise. He could feel it, both inside his body and on his skin. The thick blood vessels across his body pulsed, and with each heartbeat came more power. With a single heave, Davis pushed Wilcox off of him and got to his feet.

Wilcox backed away laughing. "So you do feel the power. You've become just like me."

Davis sneered as he moved to engage Wilcox. "No, not like you. You're just a watered down version of me."

He slammed his fist into the skin side of Wilcox's face, collapsing the bone around the eye and squashing the orb so that it hung by its nerve. The next punch broke through Wilcox's teeth and popped the jaw bone out of place. Davis shoved his fist down Wilcox's throat, and he coiled his fingers around the squirming, slimy tongue.

With one hand, Davis pushed Wilcox away, and with the other he pulled the tongue towards himself, like tug-of-war with the general as the rope. Wilcox screamed and clawed at Davis, but Davis ignored the breaking of his own skin. Wilcox's one good eye spun like a dying top while the other bobbled up and down.

Davis put every ounce of effort he had into his hand, feeling his fingernails tear through the tongue muscle. Thick streams of blood flowed out from between Wilcox's splintered teeth. With a final yank and a sound like tearing fabric, Davis pulled the tongue free from Wilcox's face.

Wilcox grabbed at his mouth, trying to stem the gushing of gore from deep in his throat. Davis waited until the loss of blood dropped the general to the ground.

Wilcox's veins still stuck out on his skin, but they were still and lifeless. The body twitched, and the eyeball stared at Davis. Davis didn't want it to be quick. He put his foot down on Wilcox's head, just as Wilcox had done moments earlier, and slowly applied pressure. Bones snapped and started to creak and crackle as they grated against each other. Wilcox made one last effort to pull Davis's leg away, then the skull crumpled like a wet cardboard box.

Davis chucked the tongue away and shook the brains off his foot. He shrugged. So much for Wilcox.

He stood over the crystal, blood dripping from his face and landing on the alien object where it slid smoothly off. The blood could have been his or Wilcox's, but he didn't care. He picked up the crystal with the intent of grabbing a heavy object. The crystal was so light that Davis almost tossed it into the air on accident.

He found a patch of land relatively free of zombie parts. It was nothing but empty concrete and a perfect place to break the crystal. He brought the rock overhead and then slammed it down as hard as he could.

The crystal didn't even bounce. It stuck to the ground and stayed there. Unbroken.

Davis tried again several more times, each attempt yielding the same result. Crushing the crystal crossed Davis's mind, but his gut told him he'd get the same outcome. It was an extraterrestrial object made from alien technology. Wilcox was right. Davis couldn't understand the crystal.

But he couldn't just throw it away. If the zombies found it once, they could find it again. He had to keep it with him, but as long as he did that, the zombies would come for him. Either choice made for an unpleasant future for him.

His thoughts occupied him so much that it was almost too late before he noticed someone in the distance running in his direction. Leaving the crystal where it lay, he jumped onto a pile of bodies and waited. He wanted to get the jump on whoever it was.

As the person approached, he recognized her.

"Jacey," he shouted.

She screamed and socked him in the mouth.

Davis tried to wipe the blood off his face. "It's me. Don't you recognize me?"

Jacey took a few moments to look through the grime on Davis's face. At the same time, they said "What are you doing here?"

Jacey answered first. "It doesn't matter. This place isn't safe. Zombies are fighting aliens. Aliens are fighting aliens. I think I'm going crazy."

"Well, don't go crazy yet. I need you to find a car to make an escape. Can you hot wire a car?"

"I don't even know how to drive."

Davis patted her on the shoulder with a bloody hand. "You'll figure it out."

"What are you going to do?"

"I have to find someone. Take care of some things."

"Get yourself killed."

"Maybe. If you need to escape without me, go ahead. You don't owe me anything."

Jacey smiled. "But if I save you, you'd owe me two favors."

"Just get going."

Jacey started to run, slowly at first as if she were waiting for Davis to join her, then she darted off. Davis wondered if he should have given her the crystal but thought that it would put her in too much danger.

He picked up the crystal and tucked it under his arm as he started down the path that Jacey came from. All the action was probably in that direction. Maybe there were some answers there, too.

# CHAPTER TWENTY-EIGHT

The darkness had its hold over the Vicious One.

The wounds, both external and internal, all over the Vicious One let it know that it should have been dead long ago, that it should not have been able to stand up against the warrior for so long. The Vicious One was broken, and it was not healing, yet it still found that it had power over its muscles and that it could continue the fight.

But that was less of a concern to the Vicious One compared to the effects that the darkness had on its soul. There was a cloud over its mind, hiding what it thought it knew about itself. As every moment passed, that cloud grew thicker, and the Vicious One knew that it could fade into nothingness and meld with the darkness. Only its intense focus kept it from losing its identity.

And from somewhere deep in that cloud it heard something, a voice. It was just a whisper, yet it was louder than any noise from the environment. And it spoke the Vicious One's secret name. It only had to answer that call, and it would surrender itself to the darkness. Become a slave to the Others.

The Vicious One dodged out of the way as the warrior slammed its fists into the ground, cracking the solid substrate. The Vicious One slashed at the warrior's face, digging deep enough to leave marks on the skull.

The Pious One came in again with the gravity drive and hammered it into the warrior's torso. Ribs cracked so loudly that the sound could be heard and felt. The warrior pummeled the Pious One who only saved itself by using the gravity drive as a shield.

A loose armor plate flapped on the warrior's carapace, and the Vicious One grabbed a hold of it and yanked on it, peeling it off and exposing thick cords of striated muscle. Turning the armor piece around, the Vicious One jammed the jagged edge into the muscle. Strands broke apart and snapped with the release of tension, and the Vicious One shoved the armor in deeper until it felt the weak resistance of the warrior's organs.

The Vicious One tossed away the armor piece. The open cavity on the warrior's back released a noxious blast of putrefying gases that burned the Vicious One's remaining eye. It ignored the pain and dug its hand inside, breaking through the rotten membranes surrounding organs and mashing the warrior's guts into pulp.

The warrior ended its attack on the Pious One and tried to shake the Vicious One off. With its free hand, the Vicious One dug its claws into the warrior's skin and latched its jaws onto the back of the warrior's shoulder. No matter how hard the warrior tried to remove its pest, the Vicious One held on.

The Pious One swung the gravity drive back and forth into the warrior's face. Each blow sent the warrior's head snapping to either side, and more and more of its decomposing flesh stripped off until nothing was left but its deformed skull.

With a violent surge, the warrior escaped from the reach of the Pious One and the gravity drive and purposefully flopped onto its back. The Vicious One was caught between the hard ground and the warrior's harder carapace. Under the crushing pressure, a thick gob of blood gushed out of the Vicious One's mouth and ran into its eye.

Its vision became only blackness, and it thought that it had finally joined the Others. It felt peace and calm, and a sense that it was one with the rest of the species. It was a sense of safety that it had never experienced before. And then the voice called out its secret name.

The Vicious One knew that it was all a falsehood. As long as it was able to resist, it would never succumb to the darkness.

Life returned to it, and the hand it had jammed inside the warrior's body restarted its destructive movements. The warrior let out an insane howl as the mix of blood, guts, and juices seeped out of the hole in its back.

The Pious One jumped onto the warrior's chest and held the gravity drive high over its head. The pillar came down like a meteor onto the warrior's skull.

The Vicious One squirmed its way out from under the warrior's body. The warrior crawled away, leaving a trail of brains. It no longer had any fight left in it, and the Pious One could have finished it at any moment.

The warrior spoke telepathically. 'You think you have won, but I sense that my infected slaves have killed the rest of your comrades. And how far do you think you can run before my human servants find you? The gravity drive will soon belong to us, and the rest of the species will join us.'

The Pious One made a move to kill the warrior, but the Vicious One held up a hand to stop it.

The warrior continued. 'The end may even be sooner than you think. The gravity drive's power source is here.'

In the distance, a human, carrying the power source, stood calmly. The woman and her followers faced him, their relaxed poses an instant away from turning to fighting stances. The Vicious One recognized the distant human as the corrupted one that had freed it from its chains. Even with the darkness flowing inside of him, that human was no friend of the Others. Why was he bringing the power source to them?

A horde of the infected slowly crept into view, trapping the man between them and the corrupted, but the man did not act like he cared.

The Vicious One had no time to ponder human motivations. It had to prevent the gravity drive and the power source from ever meeting. It turned to the Pious One. 'Kill this unfaithful coward.'

With the gravity drive, the Pious One sent a powerful stroke towards the warrior's shattered skull and obliterated its unnatural life.

'We cannot allow the corrupted to get that power source,' said the Vicious One. It took a step and felt broken leg bones grind against each other. There was no pain. There wasn't even a loss of strength. It wondered what it would feel like once its flesh started rotting.

'The infection has spread?' asked the Pious One.

'The infection has completely taken over,' replied the Vicious One. 'We cannot let that distract us from our mission.' The voice calling inside the Vicious One's head begged to differ.

The man holding the power source continued his face-off with the corrupted humans. The woman stood closer to the man than the rest of her companions, and she seemed to share a bond with the man.

All this proved to be a significant distraction for the Vicious One and the Pious One. The corrupted focused so intently on the man, and probably believed too much in the strength of the warrior, to think that the Vicious One and the Pious One could pose a threat. The man made sure that the corrupted humans kept their eyes on him.

They attacked, taking advantage of the surprise to gut several of the corrupted before they had a chance to react. Several fell within a matter of moments.

The woman lunged at the man, but the Vicious One snatched her out of mid-air and hurled her towards the infected. A corrupted tried to jump on the Vicious One, but the Pious One batted it down, the impact splitting open the human's abdomen.

Then the horde charged. The Vicious One could not guess their numbers. There were far too many for it and the Pious One to have any hope of success. The only thing it could do was kill.

With tooth and claw, the Vicious One ripped and tore and smashed and crushed until the very air it breathed hung thick with blood particles and the ground was a red slop. The unnatural strength given to it by the corruption powered every attack and pushed its strength and endurance beyond what it thought possible.

Heaving the gravity drive as a weapon, the Pious One cleared large swathes of area of the infected. It fought as one who's mind and body had merged into one, the purity of its strength matching the Vicious One's polluted strength.

The infected had two targets. They split up, half taking the Vicious One and the Pious One, and the other half taking the corrupted man. He battled against the woman and the infected alike, struggling to keep a hold of the power source, and though rage kept him in the fight, he was losing ground to his enemies.

The Vicious One had to take the power source from the man. If the human fell, the power source would belong to the Others. Maybe there was a chance that the Pious One could escape with the gravity drive and the power source? Then it could find some way to destroy them both.

The Vicious One tried to stampede through the crowd of infected, but there were so many it was as if they formed an impenetrable wall. They clambered onto the Vicious One and brought it to the ground where they started to eat into its flesh.

The darkness started descending on the Vicious One again. It needed to keep fighting, but it just could not find it within itself to go on. The voice beckoned ever louder, and the temptation to answer was overwhelming.

A high pitched noise, some kind of honking sound, blared over the voice in the Vicious One's head. The honking continued in short blasts, and then a vehicle plowed through the infected and stopped near the human man.

A human female stepped out of the vehicle. The Vicious One recognized her, but its mind was too far gone to draw up the memory. This new woman carried a gun and started shooting indiscriminately into the infected. She did not appear to know how to use the weapon, but the sheer number of targets available made that point irrelevant. She tossed a second weapon to the man and together they started destroying infected.

The Vicious One did not understand. Why did that woman come to rescue the man? Her planet was about to be overrun with the infected. Survival instincts dictated that she should find some way to avoid the infected, to accept that she, a single human, could not possibly change anything. Her only option was to run, and yet she risked her life, risked the chance of becoming infected, to come here and fight.

The voice in the Vicious One's head told it that it did not need to understand. The Vicious One ignored the voice.

Knowing that it would be performing its final act, the Vicious One threw off the infected covering its body and shredded the ones that remained. It cleared a path through the infected until it stood with the Pious One.

Over the cries of battle, the Vicious One spoke. 'Give me the gravity drive.'

The Pious One continued to crush the infected around it. 'What for?'

'I am going to bring our species to this planet.'

Without a response, the Pious One swung the gravity drive at the Vicious One. The Vicious One narrowly dodged the blow. 'You will destroy us!'

'No. Our species will fight and rid the galaxy of its darkness forever. We will endure.'

The Pious One batted away several advancing infected but did not answer.

'Our species died a long time ago,' said the Vicious One as it battled the infected. 'We decided to hide in the vastness of space instead of fighting. Now is the time we reverse that decision. It is on this planet where we will learn if we are masters of our fates or if we have been slaves to the Others all along.'

The Vicious One sensed that the Pious One's mood shifted. It destroyed an infected then handed the gravity drive to the Vicious One.

'You owe me your life,' said the Vicious One. 'I order you to flee this battle and await the arrival of our species. Then you will lead them to victory.'

The Pious One glanced quickly at the Vicious One. 'Yes,' it said and ran off. It dove into the ocean and disappeared.

The gravity drive proved a useful weapon against the infected, and the Vicious One crushed them under the device until it stood in the circle the man and his friend cleared out with their guns.

The man stared up at the Vicious One, but he did not attack. In one hand he held his gun. In the other he held the power source.

The Vicious One held its empty hand out to the man.

# CHAPTER TWENTY-NINE

The beating of his heart and the blood rushing through his brain was almost as loud as the clash between the aliens next to the navy ship. Even from a distance, Davis could tell that the fight was bloody.

The aliens fought with a ferocity unmatched by the forces of nature. Or at least nature as it was known on Earth. Davis had never seen such power, and he wondered if the zombie infection within him would give him that power. He only wanted a little bit. Just enough to defeat Elise and her friends.

The crystal fit comfortably under his arm, so Davis knew that the uncontrollable shaking in his hand was not from the weight of the rock. He squeezed his fists several times to try to get them to stop shaking. As his muscles tightened, his veins formed shallow ridges on his skin. Zombie veins, Davis thought. He relaxed his hands. The shaking didn't stop, but the veins receded.

Elise caught his arrival, and she and her flunkies headed towards Davis. Halley was with them. His stump dripped freely, and his face had gone ghostly pale. He could have passed out or died at a moment's notice he looked so sick.

Elise pointed at someone. "Get the major out of here," she said. One of her people obeyed and prodded Halley to pick up his pace. Halley glanced at Davis, but Davis couldn't tell if it was a plea for help or just the loss of blood that put the pain in Halley's eyes. With another prod, Halley stepped faster, and he and his captor or ally disappeared behind a shipping container.

Davis's eyes followed Halley, then he saw the massive army of zombies assembled behind him, trapping him. They were silent. No groans, no growls.

"It's very kind of you to bring us what we need," said Elise.

Davis hoisted up the crystal. "It's not a gift. You know, I don't even know what it is."

"That is the power source to a device that will bring their kind to Earth." She turned around to gaze at the fighting aliens. Their battle had turned into a wrestling match. "When they arrive, that will be the first day of the galaxy's glorious future."

"And if I don't give you this thing?"

"You will give it to us. We have unleashed the zombie plague on the world. It is more potent than the last time. Humanity barely survived the first war. It won't survive a second."

Anger sparked in Davis's mind. Humanity would survive. He knew it. Davis wanted to hurl the crystal into Elise's face. "What's your point?" he asked.

"There is no nuclear device or chemical formula that can kill the zombies. Humans are weak. The alien species is the only thing powerful enough to defeat the zombies."

"So you infected the earth just to force my hand into giving you this crystal? And then you turn the aliens into zombie aliens? Is that it?"

Elise smiled and stepped closer to Davis. "Zombie aliens. I like that. When their species is corrupted, they rise to a higher plane of existence. They become transcendent. They touch god, or whatever you want to call it."

Elise and her friends all faced Davis. He was the only one that saw the small alien crush the head of the monstrous one. One of the aliens struggled to its feet, and then they started walking towards the group of assembled humans. Elise's friends glared at Davis, and Davis made sure to return their glares. Anything to keep their eyes on him and not on the aliens behind them.

"Maybe I'll give you this thing in exchange for answers," Davis said. "Why am I immune to the zombies?"

"There are many people like us," said Elise. "It's in our DNA. We are the chosen few who will be joining the aliens in their transcendence." She held her hands out for the crystal. The aliens grew nearer.

"Why were we chosen?" asked Davis, but Elise didn't respond. "What happened in the forest when I was attacked by the zombies?" Elise only had to open her mouth and the truth would be known. Davis spoke again. "Why did you leave me?"

Elise smirked like a little kid that enjoyed keeping a secret, enjoyed torturing Davis with something he would never know.

Everyday that he sat in his cell, Davis wanted to know what happened to him. What memories he had lost. Looking at Elise and that smile of hers and the evil gleam in her eye, that desire vanished. Was Elise evil back in the war? Was he? Maybe he was, but losing his memory meant that he was free from his past. He could build his own future.

He knew he wouldn't get his answers, and he knew those answers wouldn't mean anything. And in a few seconds, nothing would matter.

"You know what?" Davis said, shrugging his shoulders. "Fuck it."

The aliens pounced on Elise's allies, quickly rending several of them limb from limb. Their blood squirted in the air and rained down over Davis and Elise.

Davis drove his foot into Elise's gut, and the feeling of his foot sinking into her satisfied him to no end. She wasn't faster than him anymore.

Elise tumbled backwards but quickly rolled to her feet. She leapt into the air, and one of the aliens grabbed her and chucked her like a baseball. The alien looked about ready to melt into a pile of blood and guts, but it still fought with a ferocity Davis couldn't have imagined. And something deep inside of Davis told him that this was the alien he had saved earlier in the refugee city. Small universe, he thought.

His thoughts only lasted for an instant. The mass of zombies charged, and they all seemed to be heading straight for him. They filled the air with their deafening roars. Davis tucked the crystal tighter against his body and let out his own battle cry.

The zombies came crashing in with the force of a tsunami. Davis let the monster within him loose, and he felt his strength skyrocket. It allowed him to resist the surge of undead bodies and stay on his feet.

Davis didn't know if he would survive the battle, or, rather, how long it would take until the zombies brought him down. He just knew that if he wanted to hope to survive, he had to kill as many zombies as possible.

They scratched at him, bit at him, tried to break his bones and remove his flesh. He didn't let them. He swung his fist until his knuckle skin was gone and only bone remained. He gouged at eyes until his fingernails dangled like loose shingles. He smashed heads in with the crystal until he could drink zombie blood out of the air. And they kept on coming.

Defeated zombies piled up around the aliens, and gore dripped from the aliens' claws and fangs. With a single swing of their arm, they could take out four or five zombies. They killed with more efficiency and brutality than anything Davis could imagine.

Another surge of zombies threatened to engulf Davis. And through the tangle of hands trying to bring him down, despite the hundreds of hungry mouths breathing on him, Davis saw her. Elise just stood there, smiling.

"You want it? You come and get it!" Davis yelled.

Elise's smile dropped and the veins on her face swelled. A path cleared through the zombies, and Elise entered into combat with Davis.

Davis charged and hurled the crystal at Elise. The attack caught her by surprise, and the crystal smashed into her face. Her blood vessels ruptured. Bits of skin hung limply from her face, and blood pulsed from her wounds.

She dove to the ground to grab the crystal. As soon as her hand touched the crystal, Davis stomped his foot down. Hand bones splayed out beyond their natural range, and Elise's blood flowed smoothly off of the crystal.

She screamed and tried to pull away, but Davis kept his foot on her hand. "I could kill you right now," said Davis.

Elise started to respond but was interrupted by the sudden incessant honking of a car horn. Zombies started flying into the air as a large truck bulldozed its way through them. The truck came dangerously closer and closer to Davis and Elise, and Elise tried even harder to get away. Davis wouldn't let her.

Rows of zombies fell like dominoes, and the truck smashed into Elise before coming to a stop. The impact sent Elise hurtling away, leaving a few of her fingers behind, stuck between Davis's foot and the crystal.

It was a military truck, probably one of Wilcox's. And Jacey sat in the driver's seat. She hopped out, dragging a massive machine gun with her. The thing was almost too big for her to carry, but she heaved it up to her hip and opened fire.

Davis expected the force from the gun to knock her down, but she stayed on her feet. Her bullets ate through the zombies, clearing out a circle around the truck. She paused for a brief second to toss a rifle over to Davis.

He grabbed the rifle and scooped up the crystal. Jacey said something that he couldn't hear over the gunfire, but he didn't need to hear it. It was easy enough to tell that she wanted to escape, and he agreed.

But despite the constant hail of gunfire, the circle of zombies slowly closed on Davis and Jacey. There was no way they could escape without a better path through the zombies. Coming in with the truck, Jacey had momentum and inertia on her side. If they tried to leave, the zombies would quickly destroy the truck and drag their bodies out kicking and screaming. There was just nothing that he and Jacey could do against this many zombies.

A sudden splash of blood hit Davis in the face. He blinked to clear his eyes and opened them to see an alien standing before him. No, not an alien. The alien. Its broken body was covered in gore, and behind it was a clear path full of ruined zombies. In one hand, it held a long pillar of stone. Its other hand was opened in front of Davis.

The alien wanted the crystal. The open hand, even coming from an alien, could only have one meaning. But why? The alien was an enemy of Elise and her cult. Why would it want the crystal? It would only doom its own kind.

Unless the alien knew that what Elise said was the truth. Only the aliens could defeat the zombies. Maybe it was true, but did humans have a chance against the aliens? Where would the war lead? Was humanity doomed no matter what?

Davis had to make a choice. Maybe, trapped in his cell, Davis didn't have a hand in building the new world. But it was still his world. He wouldn't let it go without a fight.

All these thoughts passed in mere moments. Davis put the crystal into the alien's hand.

"Jacey! Get in the car!" He nearly had to destroy his throat to be heard over the gunfire, but Jacey listened.

As soon as they shut the doors, the zombies rushed in and started rocking the truck. It would only take seconds before they tipped the thing over.

The alien swatted away zombies with its stone, then shoved the pillar into the ground. It placed the crystal on top, and it lit up with a swirl of unimaginable colors. It traced its claws over the object, and it started to glow green as the ground trembled.

Elise yelled something at the zombies, and they stood aside so that she could make her escape. Davis's eyes followed her until she was lost amongst the zombies. He had a feeling they'd meet again.

"Reverse," said Davis. "Reverse!" His insides started to shift as if he were on a roller coaster.

Jacey fumbled with the controls, then started to plow slowly through the zombies.

An intense beam of green light shot into the sky and lit everything up as if it were day. Around the device, the ground started to tremble and crack. Pieces of earth sank below the surface as if there was nothing underneath. The hole expanded wider, sucking the zombies into it. The alien fell with them, falling rubble crushing its body.

The hole started to reach towards the truck. "Move, dammit, move!" Jacey yelled at the truck. The vehicle whined in protest, but it barely moved away from the device. The ground started surging, and it suddenly felt like the truck was floating.

Then with a jolt it came back to earth and blasted away. Jacey spun the wheel, and the truck spun around.

"Just like in the movies," said Davis.

"I've never seen one," said Jacey. She laughed and gunned it.

They were clear of the city before either of them spoke. They both knew that war was coming, and the feeling in their guts was difficult to express. Jacey was too young to remember the start of the first war, and Davis didn't have any memories at all. And they both spent their lives after the war as prisoners. Everything was new to them.

"What happens next?" asked Jacey. She chuckled, probably realizing how trite her question sounded.

Davis looked outside. The green light from the alien device slowly gave way to the blackness of night. Somewhere up in those stars was an alien species that would either save the world or destroy it. Only time could tell. "We wait."

# Epilogue

The arm resting on the table in front of Halley did not look healthy. There was a bit of gangrene moldering on its cut end, and the dark veins under the skin suggested that the rot had spread to the rest of the arm. And it still moved, despite not having a body attached to it. The fingers convulsed like a dying spider, and Halley felt the vomit building in his gut.

"You can't put that thing on me," said Halley. "I'll die."

The doctor's expression didn't change. "We can do whatever we want. You gave yourself over to us."

Silently, Halley cursed himself.

The door slammed open and Elise, bandages wrapped around her head, stormed in. The bandages only left a little space for her mouth and her eyes, but the slits for her eyes were enough to show the fury within her. She held up a hand. A few fingers were missing, and only a thin layer of decaying skin covered the spindly bones. She pulled on the skin and it broke away easily.

"I need another injection," Elise said.

"It's not time," responded the doctor.

"Now."

A man walked in behind Elise. He was tall, intimidating. Maybe even royal. But his face was a ruin. Poorly grafted skin hung on one half of his face, giving him the appearance of some kind of monster ripped too early from the womb. "Give it to her," he ordered.

Fear in his eyes, the doctor nodded and took Elise aside.

The man approached Halley and held out his hand. "I don't believe we've met."

Halley tried to adjust so that his one hand could shake with the other man, but he failed. "Major Thomas Halley, sir." The formality seemed appropriate.

"It's a pleasure to meet you, Major. My name is Harrison Wolff."


Fiona stopped her vehicle to watch the green beam of light shoot into space. Whatever it was, she knew that was the official announcement that the war had started.

The last war left her with scars that she carried on the inside. The pain in her arms told her that this war already gave her scars to carry on the outside. What else would this war do to her?

She glanced back at the canisters. If she created a new weapon, would she turn out just like Cheung? Would she be able to let go of the glory she may win? Did it matter?

She had to find a way to defeat the zombies, no matter how many scars it gave her.

The beam continued through space, faster than the speed of light, until it connected with its counterpart in another part of the galaxy.

The fleet, a bunch of derelicts and monstrosities cobbled together from the parts of dead ships, assembled in the aura of the gravity drive. The distances between points in space shortened, and the ships began their flight to a planet that humans called Earth.

And deep in that Earth, something stirred. The mind and the body did not know what to make of it. All functions had ceased. They were dead. But now they weren't. And they were merged with each other and with something else. It was not a soul. It was something more powerful. It felt as if it had awakened from a spell it did not know it was under.

The Vicious One opened its eyes and joined with the Darkness.

# ABOUT THE AUTHOR

Aaron Thibault (Teebo) started writing as a young child, with the primary focus of his stories being monsters and dinosaurs eating people. And usually, the bloodier the better. In retrospect, those stories, and the accompanying illustrations, should have gotten him banned from polite society, but he managed to avoid the wrath of his fifth grade teacher and made it out alive.

He has since grown up, but it is debatable if he is an adult or not. He lives in Corona, California, and when not writing, he is reading comic books, lifting weights, or playing the classical guitar.

To learn about the latest releases, join Aaron's newsletter at http://eepurl.com/cFIe25
or scan:

www.ingramcontent.com/pod-product-compliance
Lightning Source LLC
Chambersburg PA
CBHW051243260626
47162CB00002B/572